Disappear

Lisa Landis

DEDICATION

To Eric, who encouraged me, provided some technical expertise, spent many hours discussing plot, and listened to my half-baked ideas, as well as came up with a few of his own. Thank you for being my partner in crime. Thanks to the gods for the invention of coffee—no writing could be done without it.

Grateful to Jennifer Krause, Stephanie Finne, and Erin Scott. You three bless me with your awesome editing/design abilities.

Finally, to my baby girl, Kaitlin, who thinks I am a better writer than I really am.

— Lisa Landis

ACKNOWLEDGMENTS

Lyrics from various artists, such as R.E.M, are quoted out
of admiration, all credit belongs to them.
The title was inspired by an R.E.M. song of the same name – listen
to it after you finish – it'll make sense.

Cover Design | Erin Scott

Other Books by Lisa Landis:
Waiting – under Lisa Landis Dolan

Preface-Mara

I came to disappear. I didn't choose this; no one in their right mind would purposefully make this choice. Not unless everything depended on it.

Part I

1988–Mara

Maybe now it is over. Maybe now I can move on. Todd did not take the breakup very well—neither did I. After many dates and dinners with his family and mine, I think all of us thought Todd's plans were going to come to fruition. I had sensed this strange aura from my dad as we continued to get serious, but I couldn't put my finger on it. I'm beginning to believe Dad was trying to send clues to me telepathically.

My parents are loving, wonderful people, and I have known that all my life. Even as I went through my teenage years. So many of my friends fought all the time with their parents—I just didn't. They had rules and standards, and we had our skirmishes, but even so, they gave me space and allowed me to grow up, make mistakes, and now go through heartache.

It is hard for me to believe they actually understand what I am going through. Bill and Lynne Riley have known each other since elementary school. They dated only each other through high school and college. Dad is the CFO of a medium-sized manufacturing company, and Mom is a child psychologist. Try living under that microscope! They are calm people, even when they are fighting about something; but they are both able to pop off snappy responses to each other. Not sure where my hotheadedness came from, ha!

But it has been three days since I broke it off, and the tears still come. I'm not sure I can completely define why. Of course, it wasn't a waste of time—we laughed a lot, and he truly was sweet, and I think he genuinely cared about me. I think my tears are similar to when I realized it was time to donate my stuffed animals to charity. Logically, I knew they are inanimate objects, but some little part of me believed I was hurting their feelings by giving them away. That's really how this is.

Todd is a good person. Yet for all of his sweetness, there was an anxiety and intensity about him. Some would maybe call it being Type A, a worrywart, or a perfectionist. I could see him literally freeze up over minor stuff. He tried hard to not let it show. As his studies at Boston University and work became even more intense, so did he.

"Mara, are you studying?" he asked during one of our long-distance phone calls.

"Yes, Todd. Can you stop being my parent and be my boyfriend?"

He was silent for a minute, and then I could hear the edginess in his voice. He said, "Mara, you know this is important. You know you're going to have to have the grades to make it into Boston University. Have you started your essay portion yet?"

I sighed, knowing I needed to finally say something. "Todd, I'm not going to BU."

Silence.

"Hello, Todd? Hey, I know this is what we thought we wanted, but I've been looking at a lot of schools, and I've just been having fun with friends, like seniors are supposed to, and well, a lot of them are going to Northwestern, so that's where I'm applying first. It really has a better Journalism program than BU. I'll be a little closer, and it will be easy to fly back and forth from Chicago to Boston."

Still silence.

"Todd, are you listening? What's wrong?"

He exhaled and then said very evenly, "Mara, that isn't part of the plan."

"We, or really, you, made this plan some time ago. Things change. That doesn't mean everything changes."

"Boston puts you here."

I replied, starting to get annoyed, "Why do I have to go there? After all, it was you who left, who chose to go far away."

"What is the matter with you, Mara?" His voice was getting tight with anger. He stopped, trying to regain control.

He then changed his tone, trying to sound like a nurturing parent to a child. He calmly said, "Has something happened to upset you? Just tell me what is upsetting you."

I took the bait, "Okay, for starters, I'm sick of being the odd person out of EVERYTHING. My weekends are boring. All I do is work and study, and I'm sick of it. I just want to have some fun!" I was yelling, much to my surprise and obviously his.

"You need to knock this off and start acting like a grown woman," he retorted sternly.

"Excuse me? I'm acting like an eighteen-year-old who wants a life before it all becomes about work. I'm sorry you don't get that!"

"Oh, I get it all right," he said, the sneer clearly in his tone. "You think your pretty face alone will guarantee success? It most certainly will not. You really want to equate yourself with immature fools?"

"They. Are. My. Friends."

"And would those be the same friends who got you drunk a couple of months ago?"

Now it was my turn to go silent. Todd did not tolerate alcohol or tobacco use. Yes, I did get drunk, and it was fun, but we were safe and everything was fine. I kept it a secret because I knew he would be furious. So how did he know?

"Your silence implicates," he said, in a holier-than-thou manner.

I went back on the offensive. "Fine, yes, I did. How did we get here from a conversation about where I'm going to college?"

"It's the beginning of a bad path. You're not paying attention. It's these kinds of ridiculous events that take us away from the results we've been planning."

Now I'm just pissed. "You know what, Todd? It was scary, spooky, crazy to formulate your little plan when I was just 16! And you expect to keep me under your thumb? I have plans and dreams too, and I won't be your accessory-doll-girlfriend-wife, whatever you call it. I am DONE! As in, I'm a free person, I belong to NO ONE, and I do not belong to you!" Wow. That felt good.

There was another one of his controlled silences that lasted a full minute. In that moment, I resolved to be stubbornly silent too. And then it came, first a chuckle.

He said, "Mara, you really are an obtuse child at times. Temper tantrums don't suit you. But, fine. You want to explore the world?" he asked sarcastically. "You go do that. But do not think for a moment that I will take a drunken whore as my wife. You end it now, you never can return, do you understand? I'll give you until tomorrow to cool off and to remember that every hour I have worked in school and at this job has been toward our life plan, for you, for us. Maybe you'll find some gratitude. I expect to hear from you tomorrow afternoon with an apology. Or don't call at all."

With that, he hung up, and I was stunned. My heart raced and tears welled up. I think I just broke up with him. I expected him to apologize. All at once, I was angry, bewildered, and yet strangely satisfied.

After crying for several minutes, I realized I never discovered how he knew I had gone out and gotten drunk with my friends. I mean, it was just us four girls at Melody's house. Her parents were out of town, and she got her older brother to buy us a few bottles of wine. It was a beautiful night, we sat out on the front porch, listening to music, giggling, but trying not to be noisy. It wasn't like this was something we did often. But the opportunity had presented itself.

We all spent the night; our parents knew where we were—they just didn't know that Melody's parents were gone.

After polishing off two bottles of wine, we moved to the front porch with another bottle of wine. Jackie even pulled out a pack of cigarettes—I had smoked a couple of times before and I could take it or leave it, but with the wine and the girls, I gladly reached for one. I was so happy to be with Jackie, Melody, and Jennifer, relaxing and having fun. I paid no attention to anyone who drove or walked by. We were smart enough to not have any lights on and to be careful from being too noisy. So how did Todd know?

1999–John

Who doesn't believe in the power of Etta James's "At Last"? It's a song for those of us who dated a lot or who have been brokenhearted one too many times. That was the song that rushed to my brain when I found myself completely and wholly in love with Mara Riley.

Mara is the most amazing woman I have ever been with, and later today, I'm proposing to her. Not by bended knee, as I knew that would irritate her—she isn't a cliché romance kind of gal. What wasn't cliché, and was the right thing to do, was sitting down with her parents to announce my intentions. I love them to pieces. Last year, they met my parents, Michael and Sheila Finegan, and have since become friends, which is so cool.

I wasn't seeking permission, but deeply seated traditions—especially of two Irish families—cannot be eradicated. Mara's dad, Bill, took the opportunity to let me have it by teasing me incessantly. "My daughter is still a virgin, right? She isn't pregnant or anything?" and "Do you actually feel you can support her?" Meanwhile, Bill's bride of thirty-four years, Lynne, laughed and rolled her eyes at him in that knowing way that only a couple with that much longevity can do.

Mara has a younger brother, Andrew, who has already been married for three years to Katy, and they are expecting their first child in about three months or so. I wanted to hold off on the proposal to not take away from their big day, but I wanted to enjoy the spotlight for a little while before the baby was born—that and I didn't think I could hold out much longer.

I'm child number three of four. My siblings—Sean, Mallory, and Kayla—are all married. Between them, they have my parents busy with six grandchildren, yet they've still had time to pressure me into "settling down."

Usually, the third Sunday of the month is family dinner at my folks' place. For the last three months, Mara has joined us, finally accepting the invitation my mother gave her after our first couple of months together. Mara has a strong sense of family—maybe even more so than I do because hers is smaller—and she didn't want to butt in on our tradition until she was more familiar with my crew.

To illustrate how funny that was to me, if Mom saw the garbage man walking by, looking lonely, she would invite him in for dinner. I swear, we are *the* most informal, communal family I know; we are very much a room-for-everyone-no-one-should-be-alone type of family. To me, it defines Christianity better than half of the crap preached at church. My parents aren't naïve, but they have soft hearts. I didn't always think it was cool that they had such an open door, but as a teenager, I slowly realized our place was where all our friends wanted to hang. It wasn't like we didn't have rules, nor did my parents try to be hip and relate. They're just caring people who respected us as people too and didn't look down at us because we were teenagers.

For last month's family Sunday dinner, Mara pleaded with me to go even though she was sick and staying home. I know this may sound corny, but we still had separate places. We didn't want to rush things by "moving in," even if one of us was at the other's a couple nights a week—it was still separate.

I thought this dinner would be the right time to talk to the family. If one could get the attention of this crazy clan. "Hey, Mom, Dad, everyone," I raised my voice over the melodic hum of conversation, "can I have a moment?" There were a few wisecracks from the peanut gallery. "Oh hush, Johnny wants his turn," Mallory said playfully.

"What is it John-John? Another movie or restaurant review to enlighten those of us not living the glamorous bachelor life?" Sean teased from three seats down.

"All right, ha-ha, chill everyone. I actually have something serious to talk about," I said, attempting a straight face, though I'm bursting inside.

"Oh, Johnny, is everything okay at work?" Mom asked. She is such a worrier sometimes.

"All good."

"Did something break down at the apartment?" Dad asked.

"No. No more talking, no more questions," I took a deep breath before saying, "So, I made an investment." I saw mouths opening and quickly said, "No . . . no talking." I pulled out the black box from my pocket that had the one carat princess cut diamond on a platinum band studded with petite diamonds and open it for everyone to see.

"I'm asking Mara to marry me this next weekend."

There was a quiet never heard in the Finegan household, and then the room erupted with an ear-splitting mix of high-pitched screams from my sisters and sisters-in-law and a "HOO RA" from Sean and Mallory's husband, Jay, both former Marines. Suddenly, I was smothered by Mom, and I felt her tears of joy on my cheeks.

"Sheila, good grief, unhinge from the boy so I can give him a hug too," Dad pleaded.

Is there anything better than the love, joy, support, and elation of your family?

Even after Mom served pecan pie, I was still answering questions. Finally, I surrendered. "Let's see if she says yes. But seriously, I'm banning all of you from talking to her because you people suck at keeping a secret."

There was laughter all around. Kayla feigned hurt feelings, saying, "Johnny, not fair. You know Mara and I go to that same aerobics class together. She's going to think I'm blowing her off."

"You ARE!" I shouted emphatically, though smiling. "Deal with it. One week. That's all I'm asking."

Mom was smiling nonstop, as if the expression was to be a permanent fixture on her face. While Dad and Kayla's husband, Eli, were washing and drying the dishes, Mom sat by me on the couch, her fingers absently, yet lovingly, running through my hair.

"I'm so happy, John. You do know how much we love and adore Mara, right?" I took her small, slightly wrinkled hand in mine. "I do," I answered. Adding, "You know, Mom, even though she's different from you, I think she has many of the traits that make you as awesome as you are."

She tilted her head down, looked in her lap for a moment, then looked back up at me with so much warmth—the kind that always made me feel so safe and cared for.

"John, first of all, thank you for the lovely compliment. You are my easy child." Then, she whispered, "It would be wrong to say favorite."

"It's okay, I won't tell the others," I whispered back, and we both smiled.

"Johnny, I don't care if Mara is a good cook or not, whether the house is perfect, and all that. I know that she loves you. I also know she has a fierce sense of herself. I like that she challenges you. I like that she isn't afraid to be who she is."

"Yeah, well, you don't see her in full-blown mad," I scoffed.

"Oh please," she rolled her eyes upward. "You don't think your dad and I go at it?"

"Well no, I mean, yeah. I know you don't blindly agree with each other on everything. But I've never seen you lose your cool with Dad—you just give him that super frosty stare," I laughed.

"Right. Because our fights are between us. But we aren't talking us. The point I'm getting to is, don't see that fire as a negative. It will make you stronger and more resolved. There will be times when you'll need to draw on that strength and resolve." She shifted positions and faced me straight on.

"Marriage is wonderful, beyond anything—even beyond your own kids." She held up her hand to shush me from mock protestations. "Kids move on, but your partner is till death do you part. The joy and the laughter are part of the foundation, but the resolve to stick it out, to not give up, is the mortar that holds it all together."

"I'm not afraid, Mom. In fact, it's the most right thing I've ever felt in my life."

She squeezed my hand, "Good! Don't ever forget it."

Part 2

Present Day—Mara

"Hey, John, is there any coffee left, or did you grab the last cup?" I ask.

John enters the kitchen with an exaggerated look of guilt on his face. "Uh, I took it. Sorry, hon.

I roll my eyes at him. "Fine, I'll just go to Espresso Yourself and fill my mug there, but you owe me," I say with false sternness.

His smile—the wide, warm smile that creates the dimples on either side of his face—always sends a little tingle over my skin. He knows that it is almost a sin to not have coffee at the ready. Both of us have stressful jobs with demanding deadlines, but we've worked hard not to bring it home with us. Even if it means staying at work late into the night in order to keep our home filled with peace and serenity.

I grab bread to make toast. "Do you want some?"

"No thanks, love. I ate one of those new energy bars they have at the gym, and it's sitting like a rock in my stomach."

"Sorry to hear that. Did you have a good workout? I wish I could've gone with you, but I was having a lovely dream about me and Mark Harmon shooting up some bad guys."

"Honestly, you watch too much of that stuff. How can you have a day filled with real-life drama and relax with *NCIS*? I don't get it," he says, shaking his head while packing his briefcase for the day.

"Mark Harmon relaxes me," I reply teasingly.

He walked around the island counter for a peck on the cheek as I am buttering my toast. "Why don't you add a little more toast for your butter there—gag!"

"It tastes good," I offer, my mouth stuffed with creamy goodness.

He snickers, shuts the clasp of his briefcase, grabs his keys, and heads to the door. "Have a good day, babe," he told me over his shoulder.

"You too, handsome."

Heading to Espresso Yourself, owned by my friend Jill Mayer, I remember stumbling on a story about a wealthy broker who was part of a Ponzi scheme. A friend of a friend of a friend's mother had ignorantly trusted the guy with the money left to her by her deceased husband. Jill told me how sad it was that this poor widow lost $250,000 and was going to have to foreclose on her home.

Now, one thing I learned early on as a journalist was the importance of tethering the excitement of getting a story with a strong dose of skepticism. Leads are great, but you cannot turn a lemon into lemonade. You can't take everyone's sob story at face value because, more often than not, the story is a consequence of a personal stupid action, and then ta-da, there is no story. You learn to harden up and let your pity meter run on low.

So, while working on other stories—you always need to have a few in the fire, as more than half of what you do gets tossed and one needs to eat—I agreed to a half-hour meeting at Jill's place with the widow, Elise Browning. I'm not a financial genius, but listening to her tale and asking hard questions warranted another meeting. At her house, I poured over her financial statements, which thankfully, were organized.

I knew enough to see that early on her returns were way above average. I researched several investment companies and their rates of return during the same time periods, and they weren't comparable at all. Of course, some funds were managed by very savvy people, and they might have a 2- to 5-percent jump other over funds at best. Elise's were 8 to 12 percent for the length of time the statements showed was uncanny. I talked to three reputable investment firms— after promising over and over that I was not investigating them but rather using them as pillars of integrity. One middle manager, Tom Prescott, spent hours with me, explaining the processes and gave me a whole new vocabulary. The pattern was that after several months of above-average returns, a subtle trend downward, and then two to six months of near-crashing levels, only then to have several months of 1 to 2 percent returns, never to get any better.

I eventually had thirty other investors from this firm with similar patterns, even though they all started their plan at different times. John Doe starts in January, has incredible returns until May or June, goes down a bit until August, crashes hard through November, and goes less than mediocre till January again. Same year, Jane Doe starts in May, has great returns until November, crashes through February, gets back to the 1- to 2 percent through March, and flatlines from there. How is the exact same plan having different results in the exact same time period? Anyway, the story got me praise and front-page status, and that jerk, Ben Levine, got arrested by the FBI and went to jail. It was so satisfying.

Reporters live on adrenaline and love the speed, but there is also great triumph when your actions lead to justice. It lasts for a few days, and then you go back to zero. You're only as good as your last story. I smile thinking about it, yet the sad thing is that for every story like that one, where you feel you have done something good, there are twenty stories that pull your heart apart and make you wonder how human beings could be so despicable.

Coming back to reality, I see Jill behind the counter and give her a wave, as she is flying around with a mug in one hand and a gallon of milk in the other. She sees me and signals hello with her eyes. A couple minutes later, she takes my purple travel mug and fills it with the dark roast of the day, which happens to be one of my favorites— an Ethiopian blend that has a hint of chocolate.

"Hey, girl! How are you?" I give her a peck on the cheek. "Good, but obviously John took the last cup this morning."

She laughs, saying, "Leave it to a man."

Her husband, Jamie, pipes in, "I heard that!"

Jill turns back to the doorway that leads to the office, storage, and dish room and calls out, "You were supposed to."

I love their banter and the ease of their marriage. I've watched, while drinking my coffee, and observed the fluidity of their movement in the narrow space where mochas are made. They've been together so long that their muscle memories anticipate each other's movements, much like the way schools of fish move— flickering, sudden, never running into each other. John and I are like that too, but in a different way. Our way is more of anticipation, of feeling, and of knowing what the other is thinking. It is sometimes a silent way of living, but it is understood, and quietly okay, safe, and absent of fear or worry. I know when to leave him alone, and he knows when to let me ride out problems that I'll eventually talk to him about, instead of trying to fix them. He is my peace of mind. We couldn't possibly be in the same line of work together, as we each need to run the show. It amazes me how Jill and Jamie do it.

As I sip my coffee, enjoying the flurry of activity around me, I pull out my tablet and start going over notes for a new piece I'm working on. There is nothing adventurous or exciting about it—a simple exposé on the new OSHA regulations and the effects on some of our local manufacturers. I don't pick or make news, I report it. Occasionally, it really bugs the hell out of me, seeing where journalism is going. It seems hyper, more opinionated, and less accurate than ever before. I often question why I continue. The pay isn't great, the general public doesn't seem to rely on or care about truth anymore, and my patience and tolerance are starting to wear thin, as people are less willing to be sources for fear of someone suing them over something.

After an hour of reviewing my notes, I get a text from Eric: "I think I have something new for you, Mara."

Eric is one of my confidential informers. He is a bit paranoid, but the precise information he provides is amazing. It's probably good we haven't met in person, but I have come to trust him implicitly. I text back: "I love how you always start with a teaser. What's up?"

Eric has been following me since I started here. Three years ago, he sent an email to my work address—all of us have an easy way for people to safely contact us with information for potential stories. I don't know much about him personally, as he is very private and very businesslike. I try to throw humor his way to continue to earn his trust and to keep him comfortable with me.

I made it clear early on that if I received good information, I would keep his anonymity, or if he wanted, attribution. However, I put the information through a rigorous test. Credibility and integrity are all a reporter has—if that is lost, the reporter is done. Bad information, unreliable sources, and a lack of accuracy will and should put a career in the grave. Eric—and I don't even know if that's his real name—has been flawless, and he has my complete trust.

New text: "Mara, this one is very serious and will require cloak and dagger on your part."

"I'm listening."

"I cannot relay over text. Go east two blocks and you will see a boutique called Ellie's—there's a package waiting for you—just tell them your name."

I laugh silently at the dramatic way Eric is presenting this new story idea, but I keep a serious tone with him. "I'll be there in a few minutes," I text.

"Good." Then he was gone.

Jill refills my coffee mug, and I slip her five bucks, grab my gear, and head out. I think the whole thing is a little strange. Eric has provided some heavy-duty intel before, and we always communicate via text. I could never go to him first, as it appeared, he always used a throwaway phone. So maybe he's getting more paranoid. What he didn't want, above anything else, is for me to attempt to identify him. But still. There was a little nagging feeling about his secrecy and the sense of urgency.

I walk into Ellie's, where an older woman, perhaps around sixty-five, with long silvery hair and dull gray eyes meets me at the counter.

"Can I help you?" she asks blandly.

"Um, yes. My name is Mara Riley, and a friend said he left a package here for me." I smile.

"Of course. Eric is a nice young man. I've never met him in person, but he buys little items here and there from our website."

Tucking that little tidbit away in the back of my mind, I realized that perhaps Eric was kind and maybe a bit sentimental. As I look around the boutique, I couldn't help but silently gag at all the knickknacky porcelain figurines. I could not possibly imagine what any man under age seventy would buy here voluntarily. But Ellie seems okay, maybe her blandness is more a reluctant surrender to her life.

"Please feel free to look around. There are some new items up by the door," she faintly said.

"Thank you, but unfortunately, I'm already running late to an appointment. I'll definitely stop back in the next time I'm in the area," I lied.

I couldn't get out fast enough; the overwhelming smell of talcum powder was permeating my senses. The package weighs about five pounds, I guess, and is neatly wrapped in brown craft paper that is tied meticulously with twine. There's no handwriting anywhere on it. I'm betting money that if I had it fingerprinted, the only prints that would show would be mine and Ellie's.

I backtrack a block and get in my car, intending to head to the office. I glance at the mysterious little box sitting in the passenger seat, daring me to open it then and there. My gut said I shouldn't open it in public. I lock my doors, turn on the car, roll down a window partway, and reach for it.

Eric sure knew how to make knots with the twine, creating a tedious task that was not well-suited with my impatient nature. It reminds me of my younger brother, Andrew, and his Boy Scout days. After fiddling with it for a couple of minutes, I pull the Swiss Army knife from my purse and let the blade rip through the knots. Though impatient with the twine, I'm more delicate with unwrapping the paper. I mean, who knows, maybe Eric is mad at me and has some poisonous powder on it. After a pause, I laugh out loud, as John's comment from the morning about watching too many *NCIS* episodes comes to mind. He knows me so well.

Inside, there were three throwaway phones, each numbered with a typed tag taped to the back. I set aside "two" and "three" and just look at "one," flipping it over a few times to check for any other markings. I look in the box for any other gifts. There was a new tablet, a driver's license with MY picture on it, and a social security card. Both cards had the name Anne Howard on them, which I know was the name of King Henry VIII's adulterous wife. There was also a key fob with two keys on it.

"What the hell?" I said. Now I was getting a little spooked.

Inside the tablet was a typed page titled "Instructions." It had several bullet points under a note that said: "Do not concern yourself with the rest of the information at this time. Please take Phone 1 and call 800-744-2277 as soon as you read this."

I look around, staring down every person walking by. He couldn't be far if he knew when I was at Jill's and then Ellie's. Not that I had a clue who to look for. I suck in my breath, power up the phone, and dial the number. After two rings, it was picked up. The voice on the other end was male, filtered through one of those mechanisms that could make the sweetest ten-year-old boy sound like a serial killer.

"Mara, I'm pleased that you have everything and called."

"Eric, what on God's green earth do you have cooking? There's an illegal driver's license with my picture but definitely not my name. How did you do this? No, wait, don't tell me. The better question is why."

"Mara, just leave the details to me. This assignment is highly secretive and dangerous. You will need to make preparations immediately. It will mean no contact with anyone, including your editor and your husband. I can ensure your safety, as long as you cooperate fully."

"Eric," I say, a little exasperated, "I don't know if you're actually a government agent or a crazy man, but I can't just drop everything and go off the grid. People, like, I don't know, my husband, will be super worried and come looking for me."

"I promise this will be your Pulitzer, your opus, Mara. And I am 100 percent positive I can keep you from harm's way. After all our time working together, have I not earned the right to be trusted?" he countered.

Try as I might not to let pride rule me, the very notion of having something Pulitzer worthy was more temptation than I knew how to resist.

"Damnit, Eric, my husband will freak out. Seriously."

He sighs. "I have to say, it's times like these that I'm glad I'm single and not tied down to another person." I also added that to my collection of observations and details about him.

"If you're willing to compromise your safety a little bit, and your husband's as well, I might add, then you can tell him you must leave immediately. However, you cannot say where and cannot communicate with him once you depart. You can tell him you will be gone for two months at the very most."

I yelled, "TWO MONTHS?! If I go AWOL that long, I won't have a job or a husband!"

"Mara, calm down. Fine. Tell only your editor and your husband the importance of this, what it is worth, but nothing more. I wouldn't mention the driver's license or the other items in the package, as it will increase the risk."

"Thank you. Can I have twenty-four hours to figure this out and commit?"

He hesitates for a moment. "Three p.m. today. Otherwise, because of timing and importance, I will be forced to seek out your competitors."

"You have others? I feel betrayed," I tease.

"Never keep all the eggs in one basket, as they say. You can call this number on this cell at three." And then he hung up.

A myriad of thoughts rush through my brain. I am logical, logistical, detail-oriented, and obsessive. They're good traits in my line of work but bad ones when I'm forced to decide quickly. I turn off the engine and pull the keys out. Maybe John will be okay if he knows the timeline; that it won't be open-ended. There wasn't a fake passport in the box, so I knew I wasn't leaving the country. My editor, Ron Cutter, will probably be more worried than John, but he'll understand better than John.

Scanning the typed note, there wasn't anything that indicated exactly where I was going; there were only miniscule details about the assignment, which annoyed me. How does Eric think I can make a decision without understanding the breadth of it? I reread the note and can't believe I completely missed one of the bullet points:

- *Infiltration of US-backed funding of human trafficking for weapons*

Holy crap. The next bullet point said to listen to a message on cell phone 2. I look at the car dash for the time and see I am going to be late for my appointment with an official at OSHA. I would have to skip going to the office. With my own phone, I call Ron and leave a message, letting him know my plans. I put all the other phones and the note back in the box and set it on the passenger's side floor for later. The appointment should only take an hour, then I can find a private spot to listen to the message and form my answer to this crazy hornet's nest Eric sent me to split open. The interview with the very stereotypical government official goes well. Dan Adams is friendly but short with his answers. These types have always challenged my ability to draw out detailed answers or something for a juicy quote—it felt like plucking an eyebrow.

While focusing on the interview, the box in my car was nagging at the back of my mind. I was eager to find out more. After shaking Adams's hand and thanking him for his help, I hoped it didn't look like I was speed walking to the car. I left another message for Ron and made my way to Lowry Hill, one of my favorite parks. It was large but heavily shrouded by immense oak and maple trees. I decided to remain in my car, as I wanted the box to be unseen.

Taking a deep breath, I pull out the phone marked 2. Once it powers up, I tap the icon for messages. It had a message labeled "Me." With a shrug, I hit play.

"Glad to know you are interested, brave Mara. Listen carefully. You can repeat the message if you must, but commit it to memory. When done, dump the phone.

"You will be driving for two days to Gardiner, Montana. Take Interstate 94 to Moorhead, Minnesota, then make your way across North Dakota to Theodore Roosevelt National Park. In Rapid City, South Dakota, there is a lodge that will have a room ready and paid for under your new name. This should be a ten- to twelve-hour drive; you need to be there by nine p.m.

"On day two, you will continue your drive on 94 to Billings, then Livingston, and a short final leg, going south on 89, directly to Gardiner. There is a Super 8, again reserved and paid for in your name. At that time, there will be a box with everything you need. Call back on phone 1 at three p.m. Directions will come from that point."

Montana. Hmmm. Not the place that came to mind for human trafficking, but I can see it. Tourists, lots of wilderness, away from major cities. The idea of being out there on my own makes me a bit nervous. What would I do for two months? I wouldn't be able to use my own credit card. I wouldn't be able to pull out any cash, lest I leave a trail. I wonder if Eric is funding this thing or if there is someone else involved. I don't even know who I'm really talking to or what I am looking for. But there are too many stories about this. It is just sickening. So many lives destroyed. And if our government is funding this insanity? It would be a huge blow of epic proportions.

My inane need for justice kicks in and I think about some cute little blonde eleven-year-old, having the light forever dimmed in her eyes, a slave to some Arabian or Indonesian pig. The more I think about it, the more my anger overtakes my concerns.

I check the time and see it is a little after noon. I need to call John, but then maybe I better just head to his office. Yeah, it would be better to do this in person, as I need to read his body language. His direct line at the firm, is number 2 on my speed dial—as wrong as it is, Ron's is number 1.

"Hey, hon, it's Mara," I say as he answered on the third ring. "Do you have a half hour for a break in the action?"

He laughs and asks, "Does that include a lunch quickie?"

I sigh. "Don't you wish? No, love, sorry. I need to talk to you about an upcoming assignment."

"Shoot. Can I make you my dessert?" I love this man. He's flexible, confident, bold, and the love of my life.

"What is the assignment? Or can you not say on the phone?" he asks in a joking manner.

"Actually, it is a fairly serious situation. Can I come over now?"

John must have sensed the stringiness of my voice, as his demeanor changed from lighthearted to one of concern. "Of course, babe. I'll ask Ed if we can move our meeting to three instead. I'm sure it will be fine. See you in a few."

I hang up, part of me wondering how to approach this with him. While he has calmed way down in the past few years regarding my travel and quirky work schedule, I know he will not be happy at all about this. And yet, while slightly anxious about the unknown, a part of me is selfishly excited at the prospect, though I know not to let it show.

I leave another message for Ron, as I am going to have to talk to him too. Then, I weave my car around the park, making my way to John's office. I can't help but continue to glance at the box. The contents themselves are innocuous enough, but yet staring at them, I feel a tug of foreboding. I usually listen wholeheartedly to my instinct, but I ignore it thinking it is just nerves.

John's office is on the sixteenth floor of the Manchester Building, a beautiful piece of architecture that was built in the early 1940s. The other tenants on the floor include a thriving patent law office and an interior design group, From Within, which is a great group of four women and two men. From Within frequently collaborate with John's company, which is called Fountainhead, named for senior partner Ed Mansfield's love for Ayn Rand. I suppose every architect feels the book provides spiritual guidance.

I don't feel my usual claustrophobia going up the elevator at Mach speed. Normally, I need to stare ahead and breathe calmly, watching intently, as the floor numbers' lights are displayed. Jenna, the receptionist, looks up as the elevator doors spring open. She greets me with her bright and familiar smile.

"Hi, Mara! Haven't seen you here in ages. You're looking fabulous," she gushes as a newly married young woman does.

I laugh. "Hi, Jenna. It's nice to see you too. How's married life treating you?"

"Ian is the best guy ever! He made me dinner last night. I'm sooooo lucky he can cook!"

I smile. "That's the way it should be. Can you tell John I'm here?"

"Totally," she says in her singsong manner, pressing her headset button. "John, Mara is here—tell her to come by more often, 'kay?"

Instead of being forced into small talk, which I normally wouldn't mind, Jenna's phone starts lighting up and she transforms back into professional mode. She is great and has been with the firm for five years. She loves people, loves being part of the team, is truly dedicated, and is way more mature than most women her age.

After all these years, I still sigh at seeing John make his way down the hallway. He's quietly confident, looking handsome in his black slacks and French blue shirt, one hand in his pocket. I always thought he could be a *GQ* cover model.

He takes my hands and draws me in for a quick peck on the cheek, then he escorts me to his corner office, which has an outstanding view of downtown Minneapolis and the first tier suburbs.

Motioning me to his mahogany leather couch, he brings me a bottled water from his mini fridge in the corner. Swear to God, this is only the second job John has had post-graduation, and he's already become a 40-percent equity partner. His office is set up for entertaining clients in a private setting, as opposed to the very public conference room near the front door. He opens his bottle of water, and sits next to me with his legs crossed and arm across the back of the couch.

"Let's hear about the new adventure," he starts.

I gulp some water, set the bottle on the zebrawood coffee table, and begin my tale. "You know my confidential resource? Well, he contacted me today with a huge lead that could shake up the White House in a horribly bad way. It involves human trafficking for weapons money."

He furrows his brow and says, "That is disgusting. Are you sure this has some legs on it?"

"Don't know," I admit. "But he hasn't led me down a bad path yet."

"True. What has you twisted up that you wanted to talk about it right now? Not that I mind having you here," he says with a devilish smile.

I put my elbows on my knees and was looking down into my lap, knowing he wasn't going to like what was coming. I inhale, face John, and say, "I have to be prepared to leave in less than 24 hours. I can't tell you where I am going, and it could be for a few weeks." Here it comes.

"What?! Are you kidding me, Mara? If it were Ron sending you off, at least I'd know where you were and that he'd have a pulse on you. No way. I'm not okay with this," he exclaims, getting red in the face. He continues, "And why the hell are you telling me here in the office and not at home? Damn it, Mara!"

John's bark has always been worse than his bite. Letting him vent would get us to calm much faster than arguing with him. He gets up from the couch and starts pacing, running his hand through his thick black hair that had just a hint of silver at the temples, then moves his hand to the back of his neck, as if massaging a bump.

"Mara, you know I truly respect your career. You know that, right?"

I nod.

"But honestly, this makes me worry. What if something happens? You'd call, right?"

And here I drop the other shoe. "John, I have to be completely and utterly undercover. That means no calls, no texts, no email, no Skype, no snail mail, nothing."

He explodes in a way I haven't seen in a long time. "Are you out of your goddamn mind?! No. Absolutely not. Not happening."

His eyes are blazing, and I thought it best just to remain silent. I know he is worried, which is sweet, but I became even more resolved to do it.

"Do you have any clue how dangerous this could be? Men who do this are sick, brutal people. If they found you out, they wouldn't hesitate to ship you out with the rest of the victims. Do you get that at all?!"

"John," I start, reaching for his hand, "I do get that. I see bad, evil things happen every day. I haven't done just fluff reporting, you know? My CI is going to be my eyes and ears, and if something goes awry, he'll get me out of it."

"That's a hell of a lot of trust for someone you've never met," he retorts sarcastically.

"That's true. However, I've never come across anyone who is as connected to everyone and everything as he is. He knows a lot of high-level government people and various law agencies, and the info he has provided in the past is uncanny. Yes, it's a little risky."

John interrupts with an eye roll and a "You think?" "But, John, why would he put me in harm's way?"

"Okay, here's one for you. Why you? If he's so connected, why doesn't he contact the police, the FBI, or whoever the hell handles this crap? They should be involved, not a reporter."

"Who says they aren't involved?"

He slaps his hand on his desk and yells, "Damn it, Mara! Why are you so obstinate? What on God's green earth is in it for you? And by God, do not say it's for a story," he warns.

I keep pushing. "But it is. And even greater than that, it's for those poor women. And, let's not forget, this could lead to the White House. Until there is solid, hard-core proof that could be a huge reason it hasn't been taken to the authorities just yet."

John stands behind his desk and grips the top of his chair, taking a minute of silence to calm down. "I'm glad you came here to tell me in person, but I can't talk to you anymore about this right now. I have a problem with a client I have to get solved. We'll talk more tonight."

I knew it was the end of the discussion for the moment. John needs his space to think out all the angles in peace before making his next move, or in this case, his next argument. More importantly, he is trying to get his emotions in check. I rise from the couch, grab my purse, and head to the door.

"Okay, good luck with the client. See you later."

"Yep."

Well that went well. I rush by the offices and barely say goodbye to Jenna on my way out. Now to tell Ron and call Eric back.

Ron sits peering over the top of his horn-rimmed glasses, his bushy eyebrows hiding his gray eyes. For two exasperating minutes, he's sat there in silence. I've learned to be patient as the cogs in his brain spin. He will not speak until he is absolutely ready to—a trait I both admire and find maddening.

"Mara, you have taken many daring steps in the pursuit of excellent truths, but this, my dear, is downright stupid."

I love Ron. He's my mentor, my conscience, and the only person unequivocally able to rip me into tiny pieces only to show me how to put myself back together again. Twenty years my senior, Ron took me under his wing when he was News Editor. He showed me the ropes, being kind yet always holding me to a higher standard and never cutting me a bit of slack. He's a hell of a lot harder on me than on the other young pups. At first, I was so upset, crying on John's shoulder, venting about how mean this guy was, and threatening to quit.

Then one day, Ron took me to lunch. After our salad and shop small talk, he said, "I don't want to hear about you bellyaching about my treatment of you ever again."

Completely unnerved, I started to speak, but he stopped me with a raised hand, "Listen here, little girl, you have potential, potential I haven't seen in a while. I believe in your ability, but you aren't going to get far unless we rid you of some of your naiveté and your sensitivity. You want big things? Well, Mara, it is a tough, ugly world out there. Washington people will eat you for breakfast, drug dealers will smell your Midwest wholesomeness a mile away, and you sure as hell won't get anyone to tell you hard truths. So, buck up, darling, or you can just move to the Features section and write about A-line dresses."

I sat silently, crushed at his slap down but at the same time completely pissed off. Gulping down my water, I found my voice. "Ron, you know I want this. More than anything. I've wanted to be exactly where I'm at now," I said, as his eyes were boring into mine. "I'm sorry I don't have the experience I probably should. I'm sorry for being a whiner, but you will not break me or scare me into thinking you are the bastard you are emulating. I've worked hard, and I'm ready to do more. I guess if it takes eating humble pie, then so be it. I want to be like you."

The corners of his mouth turned upright just a millimeter. All he said in response to my tirade was, "Atta girl, now finish your meal and let's get back to work."

The conversation gave me much to think about that day. At 26, I knew I had accomplished a big thing. I didn't want to be set out to pasture or stuck writing crap the rest of my career. I learned to swallow my pride and to turn my insecurity into determination to stick it out. I took self-defense classes to build my confidence and to be better prepared to be in harrier environments.

As Ron told me this plan was stupid, I took it in stride. "Ron, good grief, this is a once-in-a-lifetime story. How often do we get a crime like this tied to the White House?"

"Allegedly tied, but not as often as we should," he says dryly.

"Okay, what if I say I'm not asking for permission," I retort.

He sighs, rubbing his eyes. "I'd like to tell you the lawyers will not be happy, nor our insurance company, but I have a feeling you don't give a damn about that."

I smile because I know I'm going to win. Ron is management, but he is still a warrior reporter at heart. After going through the details of Eric's requirements, I could see he was very uncomfortable.

"Mara, no cell, no email, no means to reach you? This just doesn't feel right," he says, looking both cross and worried.

"Remember, I'll have communication with my CI. He isn't going to let anything happen to me. He has the place where I'll stay, knows the person I'll be taking a job with, etc. And hey, it'll give me a chance to sharpen my restaurant skills, in case you plan on firing me," I chuckle, trying to ease his mind.

"But I need to call him back really soon and get ready to roll. Just don't make Eugene your new hot reporter while I'm gone. I know he envies my desk. I see him practically drooling over it every day."

Ron rolls his eyes, "Honestly, Mara, we aren't desperate. Don't you forget, missy, you aren't the only one with skill. There are lots of starry-eyed kids out there—you aren't irreplaceable."

"Except in your heart," I tease, flashing him a toothy smile. He really is darling when he tries to be stern. I know for a fact he would do just about anything for me—he is definitely my surrogate father.

I give Ron a hug, grab my stuff, and head out the door. Ron calls after me, "Go get it, kid. And then get your ass back here!"

"Ron, I plan to haunt you the rest of my life."

———

As I hurry to my car, I glance at my watch—a beautiful platinum chain link, with a sapphire colored face, surrounded by tiny diamonds that was last year's anniversary gift from John. It was almost two-thirty. Damn it. I have to call my parents before I confirm with Eric. I throw everything on the passenger's seat, slip on my Bluetooth, and ask Siri to "call Mom mobile." I took a deep breath and waited for her to answer.

"Hi, Sweetie! How are you?" "Hi, Mom. Hey, is Pops with you?"

"Yes, are you okay? You sound rushed," she says.

"I'm rushing, and I apologize. How are you?"

"Doing well—your father and I are making a couple of dishes for an evening at the Phelps's tonight. Oh, here's your dad, I'll switch over to speaker phone."

"Mara," Dad said jovially, "how's my girl?"

"Great, Pops. Hey, I don't mean to be crisp, but I'm in a super hurry. I need to let you know something, and no, not pregnant."

They both laugh and Mom says, "Didn't think that. The prospect of you being a mom isn't the only thing we think of."

"Ha ha. Shifting gears, here's the deal. I'm about to start an assignment. All I can tell you is that it has the potential to be huge. Epic. But, I have to go undercover with no communication. No calls, texts, or email to anyone except my handler."

They are both silent for a nanosecond, and then the flood of questions come, both of them stepping over the other. After five minutes of reassuring them, I tell them I had to go.

"We love you. Please be careful," Mom says.

"Baby girl, be safe and carry that knife and pepper spray, okay?" Dad says.

"I promise, and I love you both too. Tell Andrew for me, please?"

"Of course," and then we hang up. I'm fortunate to have two loving, doting parents.

Now it is time to call Eric. I'm excited, nervous, anxious, and happy all at the same time. After scrummaging through the box for the right phone, I put my car in gear and finally leave the parking ramp, making my way home.

It rings twice. "Mara."

"I'm in," I respond as matter-of-factly as possible, trying not to let the various emotions show.

"Most excellent. Use this phone and call back at 5 p.m. I'll get the ball rolling and have everything you need sent to you via courier." Click.

During my twenty-minute ride home, I crank the music on my iPhone and sing along to Nirvana, Stone Temple Pilots, and Muse. I play loud music on my way home as my means of decompressing— to clear my head and be present for my home life. It also releases a lot of nervous energy.

I decide to stop at the gourmet grocery store and get some good cheese, bread, and a bottle of Merlot for John and I to share. Why not, right? I drool at the bakery, deciding on a turtle cheesecake, which is John's favorite. We'll eat by the fire, leaning against the couch, music playing, and it will all be good. I happily shell out the fifty-two dollars for our "last" meal, head back to the car, and carefully place my purchases on the floor of the back seat. Looking at my watch again, I see I have an hour or so before John arrives. I realize that I have a lot of packing and planning to do in that short time.

How does one pack for Montana—for the unknown? I know it can be 35 degrees in the early morning and 80 by the afternoon. Thankfully, many of our family vacations were in Colorado, Yellowstone, and other parts of Montana. I know I need enough clothes that will be temperate friendly and allow me to blend in— and I'm sure I can be okay repeating items—I don't want to pack too much. I don't want to look like a "wilderness" newbie who just got outfitted at Cabela's. Where the hell are my hiking boots? I search the bedroom closet, checking my watch to make sure I don't miss my 5 p.m. call.

Walking to the foyer, I find the boots on the floor of the front closet. I see my old flannel jacket I use when helping John shovel the snow, and take that from the closet as well.

It's been awhile since I've done any kind of "roughing" it, as John has afforded us a wonderful life—financially and in other ways, of course. It has allowed me several luxuries, such as continuing my career for the pittance I make and staying at high-end hotels when we travel. But somewhere in my DNA, I'm a natural at becoming one with nature. I start thinking of camping trips from my childhood, when I had to quickly get over peeing in the woods without toilet paper while not mistaking poisonous leaves as substitutes. I remember how accomplished I felt building my first fire at age eight; how Dad showed me the various things that were safe to eat if in a jam. It makes me smile. Obviously, I won't be staying in a tent for this venture. Nor will it be the most dangerous place I've been. I have prodded around in some of the most disgusting tenants in Chicago, so I know I'll be fine, I just need to adjust mentally. I need to get into survival mode and keep my expectations low.

I look at my left hand, which is naked except for my beautiful wedding ring. On the inside of the band is an inscription: John & Mara Finegan—Eternally. I sigh, knowing I run a risk by wearing it to Montana. Not to stereotype, but I don't imagine many of the wives in Montana are sporting French manicures and wedding rings that are as ornate as mine. I glance once more at John's token of love and devotion and pull it off my finger.

The only time I take my ring off is for certain assignments, and then it goes in a secret compartment in my computer bag so it is still with me, just not exposed. I need it. I need to feel his presence with me at all times. It was John's idea for this big ring, not mine. In fact, it was a complete surprise, which is the essence of John. He must have saved up for it for a long time, as we were living paycheck to paycheck back then. But my disciplined lover must have planned it out financially. I have no idea the cost or how long it took him to pay it off.

Two months is going to be a long time. It will probably drive me nuts to not have it there, as one of my twitchy habits is to twist it with my thumb. I won't have that comfort. But again, I remind myself, it is only for a few weeks.

I carefully place it in its original black velvet box and store it in my underwear drawer, believing this time it wouldn't even be safe in my computer bag. Rummaging through the drawer for basics to bring, as I most certainly will not need any of the hot, lacey numbers on this trip, I tuck the box under a pair of plum colored ones and put several boring pairs in a pile on the bed.

Next, I move to my sock drawer. If I'm going to be waiting tables, black ones will probably be required. I grab a bunch of those as well as white athletic ankle socks and some of my super toasty ones that are reserved for the very cold winter nights that reign over Minneapolis from December through February.

Socks, underwear, a few pairs of older jeans, sweatshirts, thermal underwear, pajamas, a couple of old painting shirts, and a few plain long-sleeved T-shirts are all piled on the bed. I hem and haw, as I need to narrow it down to fit in only one suitcase and I still have to add chargers, a digital camera, a recorder, a few pads of paper, pens, flash drives for my laptop, and my travel makeup case. From the linen closet, I pull out a bag filled with shampoos, soaps, lotions, mouthwash, floss, and toothpaste—all were collected from previous trips and hotels, because I like them, I'm cheap, and they are compact. I take a few of everything and place them in a gallon-sized plastic storage bag to prevent leakage should one burst.

I decide that even if it is my signature coffee travel mug, recognizable to many, I simply must have it. I rinse it out, place it by the coffee machine, and make a mental note to set the timer to begin brewing at three a.m., as I know I must leave around four to get a good start on the drive. I stared at the piles on the bed, hoping I haven't forgotten anything, then I decide to move on and unearth the large suitcase from the front closet.

I'm excited and antsy, not letting myself think of what it will be like to be away from John for two months. We've never been apart that long. The longest was three years ago when he traveled for work to Japan for a week. And that trip, we communicated every day. I'll miss his soft kisses goodnight—he has a ritual of kissing my eyelids, my forehead, my chin, and finally my lips, but I cannot allow myself to dwell on these things, lest I change my mind.

My head switches gears and starts feeding my ego instead. I imagine that my name is called at the Pulitzer Prize awards, and it makes me laugh at how ridiculous I'm being. About a million things have to happen first . . . still, it does have a nice ring to it. "This year's Pulitzer Prize for Investigative Reporting Excellence goes to Mara Finegan!" Loud applause. Ron hugging me as a daughter rather than his protégé, John wrapping his tux-clad arms around me in a sparkly blue dress . . .

I snap out of the mental detour and see that it is now five. I find the phone I'm supposed to use and make the call to Eric. Again, two rings.

"Mara, your punctuality, as usual, is commendable. There is a final package awaiting you at your front door as we speak. Please retrieve it, but do not open it until you are about to get behind the wheel. I'm assuming you packed accordingly, and pray God, with only one suitcase."

It isn't often that Eric makes attempts at humor, so I snicker. "Ha, ha. Yes, I'm not a novice, you know. It does creep me out that you are doing these spy-like moves like planting packages at my door, which . . ." I pause. ". . . Which begs the question: how do you know where I live?"

Now, he lets out a laugh that is half genuine, half almost sinister. "I got you a completely new identity, history, the works, and you think I cannot find out where you live?"

"Point taken. Really glad you're on my team, Eric. Remind me not to piss you off," I say jokingly, but internally, I'm still a touch unnerved.

"But of course, dear friend. We have a lovely symbiotic relationship. We need each other," he says lightly.

"Indeed. Okay, I now would like some private alone time with my husband, so kindly take your satellite, or whatever, off, please."

"Do enjoy your time—lovers' goodbyes are bittersweet. Good night, Mara." Click.

Though sometimes Eric's bossiness gets on my nerves, his exacting and extraordinary details provides the latitude that causes me to be more patient with him. I have no doubt that he probably can move satellites, and I hope he will keep his word and allow me privacy with John. My insides stir thinking about it.

Like any couple, John and I had to go through the awkwardness of our first time together, learning the ins and outs of how to best satisfy the other. He is an incredible lover, and I will always view him that way, not just as my husband. He knows how to play every nerve of my body, leaving me wanting even more of him. We are both touchy-feely people. We hold hands all the time, we hug and snuggle, and even after this long, we cannot keep our hands off each other. It isn't just sexual with us; it's part of this most divine intimacy, a melding of two distinctive individuals into one. He knows everything—he knows how I think, he reads my body language, he calms me when I'm seeing red, and he dismantles my foul moods with his soothing voice. When he makes love to me, it is to not only my body but to my soul.

He was kind enough to purchase this gorgeous deep midnight blue kimono when he took that trip to Japan. He sometimes refers to me as his geisha, which is a compliment, as I have studied that beautiful culture at great length. We are going to go there together some day. It was for yet another deadline that I could not accompany him on that trip—something I truly regret. So tonight, to ease his worry, I want to be that woman for him.

Happily, I slip the kimono over my naked self, coating my skin with the lavender lotion he so loves. The combination of the lotion and the pure silk of the robe makes every nerve ending come alive. I put my hair up in a loose bun and stick the two black lacquered chopsticks into it. Finding my charcoal eyeliner, I line my lids and under my eyes thickly. Then, I apply a bit of blush to my cheeks and paint my lips with my very bright red lipstick, becoming the Geisha. Pleased with my appearance, I find the long lighter to light several candles placed indiscriminately around the living room as well as turn on the gas fireplace. Dimming the overhead lights, the room is softly dotted by dancing yellow speckles.

I program the sound system to a classical music playlist I use for writing and romantic interludes. I hear the key turn in the front door, as John insists, I keep the house locked when I am home alone, and that sound triggers a chemical event in my body. I feel myself getting tingly and warm. John just has that effect on me.

"Mmmmm, what's this?" I hear him say as he makes his way to the living room, setting his soft leather briefcase down on the floor. Curled up on the couch, I smile and reply, "I wanted to melt away the tension from this afternoon and create a nice evening for us."

He reaches for a couple slices of cheese and sits next to me on the couch. "You definitely have set the mood nicely, though you know I'm still not happy about this whole thing."

I put my fingers to my lips, "Let's not talk about that now. Why don't you tell me about the afternoon meeting?"

Getting up to bring in the bottle of wine and two glasses, I feel him start to relax. He leans back, glass in hand, and as I use one hand to fill his glass, I lay my free hand on his thigh, my natural resting place. "It went fine, we're in that phase of discussing materials, costs, timetables, you know, the nitty-gritty before they truly commit to the project. It seems he is happy overall, which of course, makes me slightly nervous, as you know, because I think they haven't thought it all through enough."

I chuckle. "That's just like you—jaded enough to think it might be too easy." In mock indignation, he replies, "Mara, I'm wounded to think you believe that about me."

"Well then, let me take care of your wounds," I tell him softly yet deliberately, as I set my wine glass on the table. Kneeling on the couch, I caress his face and kiss him on the cheek, and then move to his soft, very kissable lips. John is a wonderful kisser—tender at times, intense and heated at others.

He opens his eyes and sets his glass on the table. "You know how to distract me, don't you?" he asks as he directs me with his hands on my hips to straddle him, as I carefully give the kimono slack so I can keep it closed, momentarily.

He runs his hands over my shoulders as I hold his head in my hands, kissing his forehead, his eyelids, his nose, his cheeks, and then back to his lips. I am delicate, barely touching. As I gently part his lips with my tongue, he puts his arms around my waist, drawing me in closer. I feel myself getting warm, and I can also feel his body come alive. After all this time together, it is still just that easy to invoke arousal and desire.

While unbuttoning the first closed button at the top of his French blue dress shirt, I slide back on his lap so that my mouth can swathe his neck in kisses. Approaching his collarbone, I use my hand to further expose it from his shirt. As I do, he slips one hand into the front of the kimono, finding my left breast, cupping it, then opening his eyes and staring into mine.

His touch to my bare skin electrifies and soothes me at the same time. How he has such power to do both has always been a wonderment to me. The way his blue eyes are in this moment—soft, kind, and gentle—it gives me the most secure feeling in the world.

It is as if nothing could ever harm me. It is this unspoken, cherished intimacy we have. So powerful. Hot and liquidy and yet cool and effervescing. Our life is such that I am at ease in his presence, the way we are in our routines—effortless, natural, and harmonious.

Time dissolves as we explore each other—joining, mating, melting into one entity. Lovemaking is just that way with John. We have an epic passion and a flooding calm. Laying on the living room floor, entwined in each other and blankets, we exhale, relaxed and spent. I look at the clock and somehow it is around 10 pm. Kissing my handsome boy on the cheek, I rise to get us something to munch on and a couple bottles of water. His hand grazes over my bottom and down my thigh as I get up. I look over my shoulder and see his sleepy smile. And it is all for me.

"Cold cuts, leftover Thai, ice cream. What's your poison?" I call through the kitchen.

"Protein. Man needs sustenance," he responds in his caveman voice.

I laugh and start plating the goods I bought at the store. Suddenly, he is there behind me, arms around my waist. "Man also needs his woman."

I turn and pop a slice of cheese in his mouth. "Eat this so you don't get dizzy, my hunter-gatherer."

He gulps down his cheese while taking a slice of apple to trace over my lips, then eating that as well. I love the simultaneous taste of the apple's sweetness and tartness, and I bring my lips to his again. He lifts me on the counter and wraps my legs around him, our bodies tightly pressed together. His hands hungrily caress my shoulders, back, and hips. He is intense, deliberate, not angry, of course, but the primal DNA of being a man comes through, as he is determined to have what belongs to him.

Carrying me off the counter, his strong arms take me to our bedroom. His eyes are wild, frantic, and animalistic, searching for cues that permit him to join us together. My body is his, and as he sees the small, inviting smile from me, he takes command. While I so deeply love his tender side, this unfettered side of him stirs me like nothing else possibly could.

Collapsing next to me, he exhales and the scent of sweat and sex engulf us both. I love that smell. Of us. We let our breathing return to normal again before either of us speaks.

"My God, man, you are amazing," I whisper in his ear as my left hand cradles his head into my chest and while the right hand massages his lower back. I never want him to leave; the after is the very best of all, our nirvana. But he does leave to use the bathroom and quick shower off. I lay there, dreamy, fulfilled, and so very happy.

The feeling dissipates a little as I take my turn in the shower, drying off, seeing that in a few hours, this all ends. I try not to let it show, as I slide under the sheets and into his arms. I turn back over to set the alarm for three a.m., hating that our time will be over soon.

"I love you, Mara," he says, eyes shut, half asleep.

"I love you too, my sweet darling," I respond, and instantly, we are asleep in the middle of the bed, in each other's arms.

—∞—

It only seems as if a minute has passed before the irritating shrill of the alarm startles me awake, my body pushing adrenaline to my heart. I leave the bed quietly, chilled by the cool air tingling my naked body. It was incredibly difficult to force myself to get up, as the weight of knowing I will be absent from John's touch is heavy on me. But it will be the fuel to get me through it, as my mind rationalizes that it will only be for a few weeks. Nothing will change, not even the season, in that amount of time.

I dress in comfy clothes for the road trip, and then I stumble to the kitchen to get a cup of coffee. I eat a bowl of granola at the dining room table, slowly, taking in my surroundings, storing them like Christmas presents in my mind, to be opened when the loneliness sets in, as it surely will.

Across the room I see our wedding picture, when we were young and glowing. There's the colorful ceramic bowl filled with rocks and shells we collected at Mission Beach in San Diego. I glance at the Georgia O'Keefe framed print of "Iris" on the wall. My eyes continue to John's leather chair, which is so old it needs to be replaced but never will be.

Finishing my granola, I linger one last time before I get up and change gears to prepare for my departure. John's hands suddenly touch my shoulders, startling me. I shut my eyes to commit the feeling of his strength to memory.

"Don't go, Mara," he says quietly, the ache clear in his voice.

I stand up, hug him, and converting to my business-like self, reply, "I have to, John. I need to be on the road in a few minutes. It will go fast, I promise you."

Very delicately, I detach myself from him to put my bowl and the coffee cup in the dishwasher. He is standing in the archway of the kitchen, arms folded and with a hurt look on his face. "Mara, something doesn't feel right about this. I have a strong sense of foreboding. I'm asking again, please don't go."

Sigh. "John, I'm not leaving the country. I'm not going on a wartime assignment. Just think of how proud you'll be of me when I accept that Pulitzer," I say brightly, trying to lift both of our spirits.

"There won't be a damn Pulitzer if you're not alive to receive it," he says acidly.

I go to him, place both of my hands on his cheeks, and look him squarely in the eyes. "I know without a doubt that my CI will not allow anything to happen to me. It will be all right. I will come back and when I do, I promise I won't take another dangerous assignment again, okay? I'll start writing about 800-thread count sheets and flower arrangements. But if I don't seize this opportunity—a rare, rare, reporter opportunity—I'll regret it for the rest of my life. Can you please understand that? I don't want your scowling face to be the memory I take with me."

Resigned and shaking his head, he enfolds me in his arms, his hand stroking my hair, planting a kiss on the top of my head. "I know. I just can't bear the thought of anything happening to you. As we get older, I get more afraid of your assignments, more afraid of losing you to something completely preventable," he continued. "Of course, there is also the risk of trying to fit your Pulitzer-winning ego in the house."

I smile. "And you don't think I don't worry when you are walking crossbeams? Absolutely, I do. Do I tell you to give it up, to not be who you were destined to be?"

"Not the same thing," he weakly counters.

"But I'm right. Darling, just trust me, trust us, trust Providence, that we will not be ripped apart. Please, love. This last one, and then you can take all the risks," I say as take his hands and kiss them. He nods and lets me pass as I scurry to do a final check before zipping the luggage shut. I then take it, the duffle bag, and the backpack to the car, and return for the box that was delivered last night.

Inside the box is a set of car keys, a Bluetooth, another throwaway phone, a GPS, and a note: "From this point on, you are Anne Howard. Throughout the drive, practice saying your new name so it becomes natural. You are a divorcee looking for a new life. You are an aspiring novelist. The #1 speed dial is me, but it is listed as "Home." Again, do NOT share this number with anyone but me. Call me when you are on the road. The keys belong to a black Jeep Cherokee that is parked at your grocery store. It has Montana license plates with GH4P1G. Leave your car there with the keys on top of the driver's side front wheel. I will ensure it is safely returned to your house. I don't want to startle your husband, but to pull this off we must erase as much of your life as possible, and we don't need anyone tracking your car and running your plates. Now begins the great adventure. —Eric."

I take the rest of the box's contents and go out to the car, dumping them on the passenger's seat, then break down the box and throw it in the recycling bin. John comes outside, dressed in jeans, a sweatshirt, and his slippers. Silently, he leans on the car, as I tell him about the car switch and that it has been arranged to have my car returned along with the reasons why.

"He certainly is thorough. But why don't I just call Bill, and we'll go pick up the car ourselves?"

I don't answer at first, then squarely looking him in the eyes, I say, "Because I don't want you to see what I am driving or which direction I'm headed. The less you know, the better."

"That is just bullshit, and most definitely reassures me."

"Let it go, love," I respond as I take hold of his hands. "Let's say our goodbyes and not make this any harder."

He tilts my chin, kissing me so softly it feels like a butterfly's wing. "Go get this. Bring the bastards down," he replies with a genuine smile and a fire in his eyes, as if we were readying to watch a Chicago Bears game.

"Yes, sir!" I tell him. And now I know we will be okay. I kiss him one more time, get in the car, and pull out of the driveway, allowing myself one last look in the rearview mirror, and I see him blowing a kiss. I stick my hand out the window and catch it.

It takes me a few minutes to find the Jeep Cherokee, as finding a black car in darkness is ridiculously hard. Once I do, I find the keys in their assigned place, and I hurriedly transfer my belongings to the back, keeping my carryall in the front with me, as well as the small snack cooler I packed. As I lock my car and place the keys above the driver's side front tire, I remember to grab the phone and the GPS. Once I make all the adjustments to the Jeep that I need, I fire up the phone and hit the #1 on speed dial.

"Good morning, Mara. Your timing is excellent. I trust you have everything and that you have left all of your identity at home?"

"Of course. Ready to be Anne Howard. I have coffee, the GPS is set, and I'm pulling out of the lot now. It should only take me a few minutes to get to the interstate."

"Perfect. Inside the console is an envelope with $2,000 in cash. Please use this for all of your expenses for the road trip. Even for gas. There are also five Visa gift cards with $1,000 on each. This is for you to use for groceries, etc. I did not want to get an actual credit or debit card with the Anne Howard name on it. We want to leave as little of a paper trail as possible."

I shake my head and smile, amazed at his ability to plan this so carefully. "You are thorough, I give you that. Though I also took $1,000 in cash from my own account."

Silence, then a sigh. "I wish you wouldn't have done that. Does John know?"

"Of course he does. I wouldn't hide that from him," I say, slightly annoyed.

Evenly, he replies, "No, you wouldn't. Actually, that will lend some credibility."

"Right," I respond, ready to be done with this call so I can enjoy the drive.

"You have a good marriage, don't you, Anne?"

"Anne? Oh, yes, right, sorry. And yes, I do. John is the love of my life." I pause, then ask, "What about you, Eric? Is there a Mrs. Eric?"

A soft laugh, indiscernible if it is melancholic or not. "A long time ago. But she and I had different visions of the future. There hasn't been anyone else. Frankly, with the work I do, I probably wouldn't be much of a soul mate."

I'm a bit surprised that he revealed anything personal but continue anyway. "I'm sorry to hear that. You know, it's never too late. I'm a hopeless romantic that way. And what work are you in, really? In all this time, you've never told me."

"Always the journalist. Nice try, Anne. It's better that you don't know. Wouldn't want to have to kill you," he says with a light laugh. While I was 99 percent sure he was kidding, I got goosebumps for some reason.

"Anne, concentrate on the drive. Please call when you make your first stop for gas and follow the GPS instructions."

Back to business. "Okay, will do. You know I'm trusting you with everything, right?"

"I promise you, if you follow directions precisely, all will be just fine," he said.

"I'll call in three to four hours." With that, I hang up.

I pull out my iPod, connect it to the Jeep's sweet stereo system, and bring up R.E.M's *Reveal* album. It's probably one of my favorite albums of theirs. Listening and relaxing, I let myself escape into the music as ribbons of orange and pink paint the eastern sky, which I occasionally glance at through the rearview mirror.

It takes a while to get out of the Cities, and I really didn't need the GPS to do so but thought I should just follow Eric's directions to the tee. If I had my druthers, I would have taken the quieter 212 route going west. Minneapolis isn't as big as Chicago or New York, but it seems so after one spends time deep in rural Minnesota. I like the countryside. It's flat and expansive, dotted by the many small towns with populations less than 1,000. These towns are Americana to me, and while annoying to constantly slow down to go through them, they are quaint and charming. There is even a certain holiness to them when I reflect that it all used to be wild, untouched land. It wasn't even that long ago, in the context of time, that Native tribes lived and hunted on these lands, primarily the Lakota, crudely known as the Sioux.

Sadly, this is not the route I get to go. Instead, I'm to keep to Interstate 94 heading west toward North Dakota. Once I get there, I could shut my eyes for the rest of the trip to Billings. I look at the gas gauge and the miles accrued and determine my first stop will be in Moorhead.

As I put my mind on autopilot, I make a point to notice the landscape. The open prairie is beautiful to me. I still see pockets of dirty, white snow here and there, as winter has exhaled its last breath for the year. I imagine if I was walking, I'd find several sets of tracks from fox, deer, rabbits, wild turkey, perhaps moose, and potentially, wolf. This land, as flat as it is, has some of the most fertile soil in the world. It is richly black, a gorgeous black. The heartland of America is aptly named. This land is responsible for feeding much of the world with corn, soybeans, and wheat—the building blocks of so much that we eat. Without the sweat of these farm families, hunger would be a constant for most of the world.

I've always marveled at how much knowledge and damn good luck farmers need to succeed. One of my childhood friends, Sara, had an aunt and uncle who owned their family's farm in rural Illinois—land that had been in her family for well over one hundred years. One summer, Sara's Aunt Justine and Uncle Darren had us both come out for three weeks to help with that year's crops. I think we were twelve—old enough to not be underfoot and a nuisance but young enough to not be obsessed with shopping malls, makeup, and boys just yet. When we were given our time off from chores, such as feeding the hens and pigs, gathering eggs, watering the vegetable garden, walking the rows to pick up stones, and other tasks, we would pretend we were pioneer women from Virginia, seeing the land before us, as we imagined they did, untouched by the modern world. We weren't allowed to make fires, as the pioneers would have for cooking, bathing, and keeping warm, but we would make lean-tos and pretend Indians were spying on us.

I look now at the fields strewn with old, rotted corn stalks, yellowy and brown, awaiting the spring plows to remove them, trying to see it the same way as I did at twelve. I wish my imagination was as wild and free as it was then. I sigh at these thoughts and notice I am approaching Sioux Falls, thirty miles left to go, and remember I'll have to call Eric when I stop.

Tipping back my coffee tumbler, I realize that I'm going to need a fill-up of coffee too. I cringe, thinking, maybe wrongly, that the last gulps may be the last really good coffee I'll have for some time. I've become a coffee snob over the years. Funny how any coffee was fine twenty years ago, and now I'm a slave to an organic dark roast. Smiling, I hear the crunch of atoms crashing against each other as my tires go over the gravel of the entrance to the gas station. The pit stop takes all of ten minutes, but I want to stretch my legs, as there is another five hours of driving until I reach today's destination in Rapid City, South Dakota, which is southwest of the Black Hills. The cool air helps to rejuvenate me as well—the lack of sleep is beginning to fog my mind. After I move the Jeep away from the pumps, I grab the cell phone, hit the speed dial for Eric, and start pacing on the gravel. He answers on the second ring, "Hello, Anne, how's the drive been so far?"

"Actually, very relaxing. It's been nice getting mental free time."

"Lovely. I would like to suggest that before you get to Rapid City, you practice being Anne, so you are flawless when you are making conversation with hotel clerks, for instance."

"No worries, I got this. But I'm curious if there's any particular reason you chose that name." I say.

"Another question, but I'll entertain it. It is common enough sounding that it won't stick in peoples' heads. But the real reason: it is a combination of the only two wives of Henry the Eighth who were executed: Anne Boelyn and Catherine Howard. Anne was the witch queen and mother of Elizabeth the First. Catherine was Henry's 'rose without a thorn,' who was twenty when she married middle-aged Henry. Her flirtatious behavior made him suspicious and insecure. It is one of my favorite historical eras," he elaborated.

Unexplainable goosebumps overcame me again, but I played it cool. "I love that era too. Kudos to you for coming up with the clever name."

"Also makes it easy for me to remember," he said nonchalantly.

"Super. If there isn't anything else, I'm ready to get back on the road. I'll let you know when I hit Rapid City," I replied, heading back to the Jeep.

"Thank you. You have a reservation at the Comfort Inn on the frontage road off the second main exit."

"Yep, I know exactly where I'm headed. It is nice to not be thinking about a deadline or anything else, for that matter."

"Safe travels, Anne." Click.

John

I can't see the taillights anymore. I keep telling myself this will be okay. Rationalizing that Mara has been on other assignments, in some damn dangerous, ugly places. She's told me about walking the projects of Chicago and seeing the seedy, inhumane sights of Las Vegas. And yet the morning's coffee is churning in my stomach because something seems all wrong about this. Mara has good instincts; she isn't naïve. She is fearless and careful who she trusts. Maybe if I knew this Eric, like I know her editor, someone I could track down and find if I had to, maybe I'd feel better. But this whole B.S. of not being able to communicate at all really pisses me off. Sometimes Mara is too confident, thinking she won't be harmed. Hyenas use trickery, wolves know their prey. The idea that we could be cut off for more than three weeks, has me completely unsettled.

It's chilly and I need to eat something to calm my stomach. I just need to get into my routine, get into my day, get distracted. Scrounging in the cupboards, I take the lazy route and pour a bowl of Mara's latest granola, though I think it is tasteless crap. I just don't feel like cooking. What I really want is Frosted Flakes as a means of rebelling against Mara's healthy plan for us; more like rebelling against her leaving.

Tucking the newspaper under my arm, I plant myself at the kitchen nook, and I have an unobstructed view of our wedding picture on the living room wall. We were so young then. I was scrawny back then, and Mara hasn't aged at all. With a bite of the honey-flavored rocks in my mouth, I set aside the newspaper and pull the wedding album off the bookshelf. Looking at the many, many, too many photos, calms me. It was such a perfect day—the beginning of the wonderful life we have now.

Mara and I met when we were both out of college, hungry to take on the world and broke as hell.

"John, you have to meet this chick who is taking over Lorraine's lease," my best friend from seventh grade, Ed Mansfield, told me. He and Lorraine were getting married in a few months and she was in the process of moving into Ed's place. It had always been weird to me how women eventually took over space. Ed wasn't whipped like some of my other married friends were, and I totally thought

Lorraine was awesome. And hot.

Ed and I graduated with degrees in architecture. We hoped someday to have our own firm, but we were slaves at different well-established companies. Ed was a design savant, whereas I tended to be more of the engineering nerd. Both aspects of the business required heady math and science skills. For a hot chick like Lorraine to love Ed for all he was, including being a tad pudgy, made her all the cooler to me.

However, it didn't qualify her to be my matchmaker. I'll admit I loved my studies so much that I didn't date often in college. I had the occasional casual date, but I haven't been all that keen on getting into a serious relationship just yet. My focus paid off. The firm that I was with seemed to believe in my abilities enough that I was named to collaborate on a serious project with one of the partners, Jack Herrod. If that went well, it would lead to more collaborations, then singular responsibilities on a project, then eventually my own projects, and my own clients.

I rolled my eyes at Ed. "Tell Lorraine I don't need her programming my love life. I'm in no rush to be tied down."

Ed laughed, "That's what they do. One gets married, and then they want all of their friends married too. We still have time left to plan a double gig—it would save a ton of dough!"

"Hilarious."

"Oh c'mon, Lorraine just wants you happy too, so that you eat your own food, instead of eating ours all the time, you lazy shit," he said, taking his basket of fries out of my reach. He then reached into his pocket and pulled out a folded note.

"What the hell is this?" I groaned.

"Dude, if I don't tell you, she is going to be pissed. And then because of my horrible memory, I had to write it all down."

It's true. Ed could recite Pi up to 32 places last time I quizzed him on it, but anything like remembering his mom's birthday, and he is a complete idiot.

"So, listen carefully," he said as I slurped down the last of my Mountain Dew. "Her name is Mara Riley. Hey—that's good, she's Irish!"

He had that stupid grin on his face. He knew my mom would prefer me to mate with a nice Irish Catholic girl and give her at least four grandchildren. Ed continued, "According to Lorraine's background check she did for the apartment, she has good credit, graduated from Northwestern in Journalism three years ago, and has a job at the *Trib* as a reporter."

I interrupted, "A reporter? I don't want to date some snotty, nosy, bossy chick!"

"God, John, wouldn't want to accuse you of stereotyping, but . . .," he accused.

"Whatever," I said, munching down the last of my hamburger, "but hurry up, I need to be back in fifteen minutes."

"No sweat. Oh, hey, here's the other note I made. Lorraine made a copy of her driver's license as part of the background check. And she used her color printer. Nice! Dark auburn hair and brown eyes. All girls lie about their weight and height, but she is cute." That dumb shit-eating grin hadn't left his face yet.

I snatched the paper. Wow. Okay. While I've always been a sucker for blue-eyed blondes, she was cute.

"What do you think now, John?"

"Call Lorraine, we need to chat."

——⊗——

That 25-year-old face has hardly changed in fourteen years. Mara isn't ravishing, but rather a natural beauty. Her eyes and her smile will forever be imprinted on my soul. I close the album and see that I have taken almost an hour down memory lane. I need to work. Everything will be fine.

I keep telling myself that.

Mara

The drive has been non-eventful so far. I'm enjoying the peace, my music, and the plains of South Dakota. It will be a couple more hours to Rapid City, which is just outside the opening to Mount Rushmore. I clearly remember a few childhood visits here and just how cool it was to imagine Laura Ingalls Wilder and her family making their way in a single covered wagon with two horses. It must have taken them weeks to make the journey. No protection from the snakes, buffalo, and suspicious Native Americans. Sleeping under the stars, unobstructed by city lights, making all of their food by fire, including coffee. Nope, I don't think I would have survived.

I both cringe and smile at the emerging memory of the one time John had me go camping with him. I was such a baby about everything that he vowed he would never take me again. It seems funny that I'll walk into a crumbling building, laden with stale urine, but I will not suffer the embarrassment of relieving myself in open woods. And I was just cold; not even John's body, a furnace in itself, could overcome the dampness from my bones. It meant I couldn't sleep, which meant I was a cranky bitch the rest of the trip.

I did make food over a fire, I did go without makeup, and I did enjoy the hiking, but once the crankiness hit, there was no finding humor or happy optimism in nature anymore for me. John didn't speak to me the whole drive back, all very long four hours of it. I felt bad. But I suppose couples find the things that separate them and learn to be okay with it. John now happily does his nature retreat with a couple of buddies every June for a week, coming back refreshed, his manhood recharged. Every couple of years, my college roommate and still best friend, Elizabeth McManus, and I go to soak sun in Clearwater, Florida, for a few days in the spring. It gives me the same thing as the nature trip does for John. I find it unthinkable that one person can be everything to another. It's healthy, in my opinion, to have activities and hobbies outside of each other. It makes me love and appreciate John more, and I know he feels the same.

The fabulous thing about a long and somewhat tedious drive is that I can go into autopilot mode, mechanically checking my speed from time to time. I can occasionally look for the signs telling me how many more miles I have left to go. It allows me uninterrupted free-flowing thinking time, almost like meditation, which I rarely have time for anymore. After this whole venture, and publishing what I hope will be an amazing story, meditation is going to have a priority again.

Instinctively, I reach for the phone to text John, to let him know where I am, but I catch myself. Being disconnected will be the hardest part of this assignment. Our evenings are generally humdrum. After both of us put in a long day, the idea of burning more energy has no appeal as we approach forty. All I want to do is have dinner, with conversation with my sweetheart, then either crash in front of the TV or jointly read in bed.

Too many couples we know have allowed work, kids, and other various obligations to overtake their nights. I realize it is harder with kids to carve out quiet together or alone time. We decided it was imperative to try hard not to dive into work stuff after dinner. I think we surprised ourselves by not having children. The timing or being mutually ready to change life so dramatically never came for us. A few years ago, I decided to get off the pill and, upon the advice of my doctor, had an easy, out-patient procedure for permanent sterilization, thus dashing the hopes of our parents. Luckily, all the siblings have filled the gap and we truly spoil our nieces and nephews. We are both perfectly happy being childless.

It's ironic, as I always thought having kids was going to be part of our plan, especially with John coming from such a large family. I assumed it would create a longing for children. My view is that having kids shouldn't feel vanilla. Meaning, I think a couple should feel ecstatic about it, and if not, they should wait or realize the reality that our species' existence is not dependent on everyone spawning.

I look at my odometer and realize that another 50 miles have just flown by, thankfully. After a few more minutes of driving, and at least five Wall Drug signs, I see that I have another 100 miles left. I cue up the 80s/90s playlist that I put together to energize me when I'm putting in long hours of writing or researching. It is beyond John's understanding how I can blast music when I'm performing these tasks.

"How does this not distract you?" he said one Saturday afternoon, as I was rocking out to Depeche Mode while constructing an outline for a story.

I took the ear pod he pulled from my ear to ask his question, smiled widely, stuck it back in my ear, shrugged, and went right back at it. I looked up, watched him walk away while shaking his head, and silently laughed to myself. We are two very different people, and I don't know why, but I find great humor in confounding him. Maybe because it makes him take himself less seriously. While the occasional button-pushing is fun, I never try to intentionally go to the point where he gets upset or agitated.

Antagonizing for response and head games are long over for me. I had to learn the hard way, by nearly driving John out the door, that it serves no purpose, and he doesn't deserve it. I can't say why I did it. Perhaps at the time, I thought any response, even anger, was better than no reaction; that at least with anger, there is an emotion, even a warped form of caring. Anger shows concern, indifference means exactly that—that you don't give a damn.

When John is drafting a proposal to its nth degree, it always takes everything out of him. He pours his heart, soul, and mind into every project, which is why he is an amazing architect. Anyway, I know that when he's in this place, it usually means he wants a quiet night, which entails a nice dinner in, lighthearted conversation, and alone time in his study until bedtime. The alone time was either for reading for pleasure or working on a jigsaw puzzle while a podcast or classical music was on in the background. It also involves two gin and tonics and a bowl of popcorn that we would split.

I know that if I want my companion back, I need to let him recharge, in his own way and on his own. I'm always able to entertain myself by watching a chick flick, working on an assignment, drawing, baking, chatting, or hanging out with friends, and in nice weather, working in my small garden. If I did go out, it would be a low-key evening because the other thing John needs is for me to be home in time for bed. We need to curl up quietly and sleep, so the next day we are raring to go again.

But one night, again, I don't know why, I was in one of my moods. I knew full well that John would be drained when he got home. He had warned me that morning that it was going to be a challenging day for him. I arrived home after he did, high as a kite because one of my stories made page three. It was the closest to the front page I had ever been, and I wanted to whoop it up. I came bursting into the door, one arm heavy with ten copies of the paper, the other arm laden with a grocery bag filled with wine, crab cakes, asparagus, a mammoth porterhouse steak, and a triple chocolate torte.

I let the keys fall on the counter, making sure there was a dry spot to place the papers. I slung my laptop case off my shoulder and started zipping around the kitchen. I waved cheerfully to John as I put items in the fridge, simultaneously uncorking the wine and pulling out various pans to get dinner started. It was quite an orchestral clatter, which must have just grated on John's nerves.

"Cripes, Mara, slow down, you're giving me a headache," he said, irritably, as he rose from the couch and entered the kitchen.

"Pardon moi," I retorted abruptly, annoyed he was killing my buzz.

He sighed, "Sorry, did something big happen today?"

"Why yes, yes it did." I tossed a paper at him and said, "Look at page three, thank you very much!"

"That's fantastic. Congrats." He came around the open-ended counter and gave me a hug and a kiss. "I'm really proud of you."

I should have just accepted that and let us move forward with the evening. But that strange thing in my brain fired up the bitchy synapse. "Gee thanks, Dad," I said too brightly.

He stepped back, a scrunched up, puzzled look on his face. "What did I say?"

"John, I am a professional—a seasoned reporter. I didn't just get an A on my homework. It was about time that something like this happened," I haughtily replied as I turned on the oven for the crab cakes while also tenderizing and applying a rub for the steak.

"Okay. I expressed I was happy for you, that's all," and he headed back toward the couch and his tumbler of gin.

I followed him, hands on hips. "You know something, you can be really patronizing at times. I know you don't think journalism is as intellectual as being an architect, but this is a huge milestone in my career. I don't need you acting as if what you do is so much nobler than what I do." I strode back to the kitchen, back to cooking our dinner.

John was right on my heels. "I don't know what is up your ass, but today has been a brutal one. I'm not going to come home to deal with you too," he shot back, his eyes blazing.

"Oh, really? I forgot that today is 'tiptoe around John' day. Forgive me, your highness, I forgot only John has emotional days at work."

"Knock it off, Mara," he said evenly but with frost in his voice. I could tell I was getting to him. I knew I started this, and I knew he did nothing wrong, but I couldn't stop myself.

"See, there you go, lordship," I continued, "thinking you can order me around." He said nothing, so I finished, "I didn't think so." I slammed the oven door and took a big gulp of wine, letting my eyes challenge his cool stare.

"Whatever," he said, and he turned to head to his office.

"So now you are going to storm off? Fabulous."

He pivoted, took a long, fast step toward me, hammered his

tumbler on the counter, and met my fiery glare within inches of my face. "I don't know why you are picking a fight, but I'm sure as hell not sticking around for this bullshit." With that, he grabbed his keys and nearly took the door off as he thundered out.

Now I was really pissed off because I had started a nice dinner and it was ruined. I shoved the steaks in a container and threw them in the fridge, then I poured another glass of wine. After a few minutes of wallowing, head bent, leaning against the counter, I paused to think about why I had ruined it. Why do I sabotage things? Why am I doing it to John?

With a deep exhale, I paced around the living room with the cordless phone in one hand and the wine glass in the other. I felt like an ass and just wanted to take it all back. I wanted a do-over. Another minute went by and then I dialed his cell phone, hoping he would answer. It rang three times, if it went to five, it would go to voice mail. He answered on the fourth ring. "What?"

Very calmly and softly, I said, "I'm sorry. I'm a pain in the ass. Please come back."

He sighed. "You are a pain in the ass." I heard the car door slam and a few seconds later, he was in the doorway, phone still at his ear. "Can we eat? I'm hungry."

I placed the phone and the wine glass down, closed the door, and enveloped him in a hug. "John, I don't know what comes over me at times, but you didn't deserve that. I can still have dinner ready in twenty to thirty minutes."

He slid his cell phone into his pocket, returned my hug, and kissed the top of my head. "You do know that when I say I'm proud, it means I'm the luckiest man to have a wife and a partner who's awesome at everything she does, right?"

My eyes met his. "I do know, yet I always have a twinge of self-doubt. It's hard to be an equal to someone who's as accomplished as you are."

"It isn't a competition. It's us against the world, not against each other. Don't ever forget that." He smiled.

"Thanks. That means a lot."

"Good, now go cook me some dinner, woman," he teased, as he playfully slapped my butt. I squealed and got to making a great dinner, loving that man with all my heart.

Most of our life together has been a dance of understanding. We each fall into wells and have our surge of quells, like any other couple, but it is rarely contentious or long-lasting. I sometimes envy that when John has a project, though it could take as long as two years to complete, he can singularly focus on that particular job. In my line of work, I occasionally feel like I constantly have to perform, that I am only as good as my last story.

Contrary to popular belief, not every story is a serious expose or part of a series or a deep investigation. It's rarely glamorous. The life cycle of most stories is twenty-four hours. While cable is killing our industry, the one benefit is we can take our time to craft the story better with our words and not rely on contextual sound bites or hardly relating video sequences. I like our process and am still a thrill-seeking junkie. But it is wearing me out. I want to do more analytical work; I want the opportunity to do work that requires more deep thought.

Maybe it's time to start that novel. I should start thinking about a good plot. While all the tragedy of real life has made me a bit jaded at the notion of a "happy ever after" story, I would like to try something happy. I want something that is believable and not as my high school English teacher called "clap trap fluff." I'm fascinated by the authors who can crank out a novel every year and somehow create a new story. Perhaps if I allowed myself more thinking time, I could do that too. I should use this drive and the time in Montana to do just that.

Really, though, as Eric said, I need to be concentrating on becoming Anne Howard. He told me to use real elements of life instead of trying to make everything up. It's too hard to sustain, and too easy to flub up and be inconsistent with details. I suppose the other trick is to not to let anyone get close enough to start inquiring about deeper details.

I think the simplest story to use is to keep my childhood the same, like where I grew up and my family. As for my reason for being there, I'll use some of my other cover up personas. I'm divorced and decided to work in Yellowstone for the summer as I get my life back together. That will be reason enough to not buy a place or sign a long lease, or more importantly, for the locals not to emotionally invest in me.

I have one more hour until Rapid City, and I'm craving a hamburger and a malt. Looks like there is a decent stop in a couple of miles. I'll grab food, and call John. Crap, can't do that. I can't call anyone. I don't want to contact Eric until I get settled in for the night. It has only been eight hours since I left, and yet it is surreal to think that just last night I was drinking wine and was wrapped in John's arms. What will it be like after eight days? What if it turns into eight weeks?

Shaking my head, I laugh at myself—always thinking ahead, always planning the contingency. I know this is a tricky assignment, but it's not like I'm being shipped out to some misogynist, Third World country. It's freaking Montana, one of my favorite places. I'm gathering information, putting together a puzzle, and then I'll present it to the authorities, write my expose, and hope I did some good.

Human trafficking is rising in the United States, even in Minneapolis. There was a ring at the Mall of America, which is so crazy, but I can see how it worked. The asswipes would pose as security guards and approach young teen girls, telling them they were caught on camera stealing, scaring the crap out of them. Then, they'd escort the girls to the "security office" for questioning, and it was all over. Makes me want to vomit.

Finally, I reach the exit with a diner. I debate if I want to eat at the diner or take it on the road so I can just be done. I decide to go inside. I put the Jeep in park and get out, feeling a twinge in my hip flexors as I stand. Geesh, I guess I need to go back to yoga. Maybe some good stretches and a bath at the hotel will help.

"Hi, hon. Here's a menu. Can I get you something to drink?" says the weathered 60ish server. She has that tan wrinkled skin and rough hands of the modern-day pioneer woman. I'll bet she has a farm and works the restaurant during the off season to supplement her income.

"Ice water would be great. And, I'm craving a burger and a malt."

She smiled and asked, "Long drive?"

"Started in Minneapolis." Shoot. Shouldn't have said that, but I doubt I have anything to worry about.

"Then the answer is yes. Let me tell you, you can get a malt anytime, but we got some fresh-baked raspberry rhubarb pie."

How does she know me? I sheepishly say, "How about both. I'll take the malt to go."

She laughs. "It's so refreshing to see a traveler eat what they want to eat, instead of worrying about calories. You only live once, right?"

"Exactly." I like her. She's like my aunt Geena.

"Okay, sugar, you relax. I'll get your water, and everything else will be up in a few minutes. How do you want your burger cooked?"

"Medium rare, please."

"Alright then," she replies as she walks off.

I like content people. Not everyone has aspirations about being a movie star or becoming a CEO of a big company. Some, like her, I bet, are perfectly happy living a drama-free life in the big country. Not that it's easy, but they don't worry about Facebook or Hollywood gossip. Which reminds me, I need to post a status. I'm very careful on Facebook; only real friends and family are allowed on my site. Over the years, I have regularly put myself on hiatus from it, whether I'm on assignment or not. It is to protect myself from speculation while I'm undercover. But because I do it often and randomly, it doesn't raise any flags. It is also why I call my parents before I go undercover, so they don't see the lack of posts and worry.

Against Eric's instructions, I brought my laptop, as I would need it to write. I had remembered to turn off the location tracker application. I'd thought about bringing it inside to take care of the post and scan the internet for news stories. I'm glad I didn't; I need to learn to unplug more often and just rely on my surroundings for entertainment.

Sometimes when I'm in waiting mode, I play an observation game. I start focusing on the people around me and invent stories about their lives. Human nature seems to require routine and repetitive processes. Rarely do people step out of their comfort zone, especially in public. So, while I don't like stereotyping, there's a reason it works, like profiling. We are self-fulfilling prophecies of how we see ourselves, so I try to be creative and imagine something quirky about the seemingly normal people in my scope of vision.

For instance, I see an elderly man having his dinner alone, but he doesn't appear sad or lonely. I envision him being a retired farmer, who left New York as a young man because he wasn't going to be satisfied with a skyscraper view of the world and needed openness.

"Here you go, hon. I double cupped the malt with ice at the bottom of the outer cup so it stays cold. Hope you enjoy it and the rest of your drive."

After 15 minutes of wolfing down my food, I look at the handwritten tab for $12 and pull out $20. I slide out of the booth, gulp down the last of the water in the glass, and wave on my way out.

My exchange with the desk clerk went pretty well. As Eric advised, I practiced saying my pseudonym over and over and made sure I had the cash and the right credit card in the front of my new wallet—a plain black one to match the non-Coach boring purse I bought. I admit, there are a few things I'm snobby about. I've already stated my coffee habit, but then there is the Coach purse. I know it isn't as big a deal anymore, as other designers have taken over the market. But most are big, bulky, and well, just completely impractical. I like to sling a purse over my neck and shoulder to keep my hands free and to keep potential muggers from a simple grab. And Coach comes out with gorgeous colors like the perfect blue-toned red, silver, and of course, purple. But the less descript I make myself, the better.

While it is only six p.m., I'm wiped out but not where I could sleep yet. I'd even say I was fidgety. There isn't anything distinguishable about the hotel—just very clean and pleasant. I've learned from all my travels how to make the hotel room coffee maker work so I can use a regular filter and my own ground coffee. One would think I'm a bit OCD on this matter. I pull out my travel hygienic/makeup bag and set it up in the bathroom and pull out pajamas and clothes for tomorrow's travels.

After washing my face and brushing my teeth, I decide to walk around the premises. I know I should call Eric and let him know I arrived, but he can wait 15 more minutes. On the side of the building there is a little playground with a swing that my adult butt can fit on. So, yes, I decide to swing for a few minutes. Why not? The breeze feels good, even if it is a cool 40 degrees. It reminds me of being ten and pretending with every up swoop that my feet were actually touching the sky. I loved that feeling. I don't even care that I'm getting the occasional perplexed stare from other guests.

After a few minutes, I hop off as a real ten-year-old is vying for the swing. I tell her to enjoy every second and to try to touch the sky. She gives me a shy smile, as her approaching mother slouches her shoulders at what appears to be relief at finding her daughter talking to another woman. I wink at the girl and head back to my room.

Propping up pillows, I settle on the bed and dial Eric. Two rings and he answers, "Anne, glad to know you made it."

"Of course, it was a good day for a drive."

"Everything at the hotel satisfactory?"

"Yes, I'm fine. Thank you for not landing me at a dump." I laugh.

"Not for my ace reporter," he responds, almost sounding light. "Tomorrow you should be able to get to Gardiner in nine to ten hours with stops. If you enter Gardiner on the GPS, it should be preprogrammed to take you around the Black Hills to Sheridan, then north to Billings and so forth. There will be plenty of opportunities for stops."

Sometimes I can't tell if Eric is being helpful or condescending. "Thank you. If you recall, I mentioned that I went to Montana a few times growing up."

"But you didn't drive it, and my job is to get you there safely in the shortest route possible."

I really didn't want to do anything else at this point but get off the call and go to bed, but I ask, "You say it's your job. Any chance I can find out who is funding this whole expedition or who you work for?"

"No comment, Anne." Then silence.

"That's all I am going to get? One day I'll break your wall."

He paused.

"You'll have more concrete information later on, I promise."

I shrugged, though, of course, he couldn't see my attempt at being nonchalant. "So be it. I'm beat and going to call it a day."

"Good night, Anne." Click.

Eric

That was close.

I will have to be more careful how I respond to Anne. All the planning. All the planning. Need to be focused. Everything is smooth now, and it must stay this way. She is still trusting. Must see this through.

I have been alone with my thoughts for too long. I've tried being good, I followed all the edicts of the Church. I was the model child my parents had hoped for; I never caused trouble. I worked hard in college, proving very skilled in the computer sciences, which really are arts in themselves—beautiful zeroes and ones coming together in perfect logic.

I've been so disciplined. My sinful side has wanted to reach for her, to just bring her into the fold of my arms. She wanted that once. Then she dismissed me. Dismissed me. So wrong, so wrong, so wrong.

I start to feel it. I must be calm. I get distracted when I let the darkness in, when I allow the anger. Yet it provides such power. Such lovely intensity. I am a man. I am a man of might. Of great intelligence. Of vigor and youth.

I know it is unavoidable to have conversations with other women, but it makes me uncomfortable. I don't like to have to report to a woman. She tries to be pleasant, but I loathe the small talk and have said that I just want to do my job.

The waiting is like the Tenth Circle of Hell. I do not understand why God has put me in this position. To show my faithfulness? Maybe it is about her worth.

Stop . . . stop . . . STOP!!!

Our time is drawing closer. Soon we will be united.

Day two, I can most likely assume will begin before seven. She is a morning person. She'll have her coffee and breakfast, shower, and then be on the road within an hour. I'll set the alarm for five just to be certain.

Check the GPS alerts again, make sure they are working properly. Put the computer to sleep, prepare coffee, set it to turn on at 4:45.

Phone is on the charger with its volume at maximum.

Good night, Anne. Peaceful slumbers to you.

Mara

The loud shrill of "Gonna Make You Sweat" by C&C Music Factory startles me upright. For a couple seconds, I don't know where I am, and then I realize that this is my alarm going off. It is my four-thirty a.m. alarm. My five a.m. one is L.L. Cool J's "Mama Said Knock You Out"; and my six a.m. one is "Extreme Ways" by Moby.

As I said, I need to be jolted awake, as I am a very deep sleeper. I also have very detailed dreams, sometimes they are even lucid. They are detailed enough that I can remember paintings on walls, the color of floors, etc. I don't always recall my dreams, like today; it felt like I took a nap and not a full seven hours of mental divergence. Sometimes my dreams will include people in my past, sometimes the dreams have symbolism, but rarely do they include John, and for the life of me, I can't figure that one out.

Hoping I didn't wake my neighbors, I get up to make some coffee and use the bathroom. I pull open the curtains a bit, and there is still a star-clad, black sky to greet me. I can't decide if I want to get ready now and get a quiet head start on the road, or if I want to goof off on my laptop, or just lay in bed for a little while longer.

What I really want to do is text or call John. Even if it were "allowed," John doesn't get up until six a.m., generally speaking. He's not one to rush around in the morning, as it messes up his methodical mindset, so he is willing to get up at six to take his time. Me, on the other hand, likes the early morning—I meditate or read or even grocery shop, which annoys John, my sweet worrier.

I think I'll peruse a Gardiner, Montana, website, to identify places of interest, know where things are. I don't want to be fumbling around too much when I get there. I grab the coffee and sit up in the bed, without the covers so I'm not tempted to fall back asleep.

There are the few blocks of convenience stores, souvenir shops, touristy, family-oriented restaurants, gas stations, bars, and hotels. But I want to know where the locals go. I go to the Better Business Bureau link and the Chamber of Commerce link and find more conventional businesses, such as real estate offices, electrician shops, one or two salons, the grocery store, the feed and seed co-op, the three veterinarian clinics, the hospital, and so forth.

I also look up the restaurant where I'll be working. It has a well-landscaped front and the typical kitschy signs to draw in the tourists. On the restaurant link, I look at the menu and hear my stomach rumbling. I know the hotel's complimentary continental breakfast is available in another half hour. I guess I'll just shower and pack up while I wait.

After a not-so-satisfying breakfast, I checked out of the hotel, having practiced my new signature several times the night before. There's a coffee shop a couple of blocks from the hotel, I recall, so after filling up the Jeep, I went there. I rolled into a parking spot and thought this might be the time to dial Eric, not overly concerned about waking him up.

Two rings. "Good morning, Anne. I hope you slept well."

"Hello, Eric. Yes, I did, thank you for arranging the hotel. I was just getting coffee and was about to hit the road," I replied.

"Is the GPS showing today's route properly?"

"Yep. Going around the Black Hills to Sheridan, then north to Billings, then to Livingston, and then Gardiner. Home sweet home," I answered.

I could have sworn I heard the faintest gasp from his end of the call. "That is absolutely correct. I am figuring another eight to nine hours today. Are you up for it?"

I snicker. "You obviously haven't traveled with my family. Road trips were a way of life. This is nothing. But hey, I spent some quality time looking up points of interest in Gardiner, like the restaurant you said I'll be working at. What I don't think we discussed is where I'll be staying. I can't believe we didn't talk about it, but you aren't having me holed up in a hotel this whole time, right? I don't think anyone would buy my moving into the neighborhood with that scenario."

"Of course not. Randy the restaurant owner will connect you with Matthew—a real estate agent. He's going to show you a couple of rentals," Eric responded.

"Super! The idea of eating out every day has really lost its charm as I get older."

"Everything will be provided. Once a week, a cleaning service will come by to keep things orderly."

I nod, even though he can't see it. "Okay. Wonderful. Anything else before I get to it?" I ask.

"No, all is going very well. Once you settle in, I think we should have our first planning session."

I'm not sure what that will entail, but I want to get going, so I let it go. "Sounds like a plan. Thank you again, and I'll talk to you later."

"Safe driving, Anne." Click. I should be used to that by now.

After getting my coffee, I climb back into the Jeep to start my drive. The entrance to the interstate is just a block away, and from the looks of it, the rest of the town is just beginning their day as well. But compared to Minneapolis, morning traffic is very mild.

Once I set the cruise control and start a soft music playlist, I float into my mind and let it wander. I'm always curious how the mind works. Many times, I find myself thinking about one thing and then I try to figure out the stream of consciousness of how I got there. I'd like to believe practicing this will keep my mind sharp and immune from Alzheimer's.

Too often my head is full with story ideas, questions, schedules, and the frequent pop-ups of errands to run, people to call, items to remember at the grocery store, picking up another USB drive, paying bills, and just the overall business of life. It is these occasions, whether I'm on an airplane or in zone mode traveling in a car, that I allow myself to drift off. Occasionally, I try to choose the topic of which to meditate upon, but that may only last a few minutes. It's not that I am scatterbrained, I just think a lot. I don't even believe John realizes the inner life I have, the sanctuary of my thoughts. But then I don't always know his either, nor do I need to know.

For being a writer, I am not always the greatest at articulating my thoughts. I know what I wish to express, but ironically, words come short of materializing my feelings. I have had to work hard on filtering myself, as I've always had a temper and have been known to blurt out whatever came to mind. Strangely, when it comes to showcasing my affection, I have a much harder time with it.

John and I have a good balance of not being disgustingly gushy and yet being capable and willing to let the other know our feelings. Some people say "I love you" as automatically or nonchalantly as "I'll be home at nine or I'm taking out the garbage." That's not my natural way of being, but it's a little more that way for John. He is the more reserved one of his family, but he does say "I love you" more than I do. His family has no maximum capacity for love; they are the biggest hearted people I know, and it did take some getting used to.

My parents have always shown my brother and I verbal and physical love, but not every conversation ends with "I love you," as seems to be the case with John's parents. I don't mind it at all. At times, when I have worked on a terribly heartbreaking story, having them and their abundant supply of care has become a soft place to land. And as my parents age, they too, have released more words and hugs. Maybe it's just me.

After too many times of being "head over heels" and getting hurt combined with my career, a layer of concrete has cured over my heart. John and his family have chipped away at it, leaving a thin veneer, which I still need so I don't cry all the time at the news I report. Once in a while, I wonder why I do what I do if I need to protect myself from it. Which leads me to why I'm on this trip. I'll readily admit my ego has a role in it. I wouldn't mind the big triumph this story could possibly bring. I do believe there is enough humanity in me that also wants this horrid injustice to end and my desire to help end it is sincere. And then seeping thoughts cascade as images of coming in contact with dispirited or frightened young women bring a tinge of nausea to my throat.

What do I think I'll find? Where will I actually begin on this? Will I have the stomach for it? Because any evidence found won't be pretty. I delude myself, at times, into thinking that if I can redirect my emotions, I'll be able to control them. As much tragedy as I have seen, I am still stunned by how evil people can be or the lengths they have gone to completely distance themselves from their victims, even though they were once innocent children at one point in their lives. Where does the change begin? There is a theory that arsonists start burning things at young ages and serial killers begin killing animals with glee and satisfaction as young as seven years old. Is it a psychosis or a gene that creates these monsters? Does a newborn babe come out of the womb with a predisposition towards pain, bloodlust, and savagery?

These kinds of questions begin to press my heart. I physically feel as if there is a foot on my chest whenever I go down this path, and I have to start counting in patterns to dispel the oncoming panic attack, like the one that is surfacing right now. After I catch my breath, my anxiety turns to anger, and after a few seconds, I look to my speedometer and see I'm going 90 miles per hour and I need to put myself in check.

Eric had talked about formulating a plan. I don't bring others into a partnership when I am investigating a story; it has the potential for danger for the story and for the relationship with said person. But this is the first time an investigation has been funded, outside of my employer. It almost makes me feel like it isn't my story, but that I'm only a conduit of exploration for Eric and whoever else is involved. While I don't like losing any element of control in an investigation, I wouldn't even be here without Eric and his cohorts' money or knowledge.

Which brings up the somewhat nagging question of what does Eric do to get the information he has given me over the past few years and this scenario especially. He mentioned it could go all the way to the White House. If that's true, then either he is an operative, a high-level government employee, or perhaps a top-notch hacker with strong conspiracy tendencies. Any of these possibilities make me slightly uncomfortable. I don't want to get entangled in some politically driven labyrinth for someone with a beef against the current administration.

American or not, I also don't want to end up cooking in some FBI or CIA pot of muck, to be left forgotten or transported to some Third World gulag. Worse yet, in a hacker's vendetta that transforms into a libelous story and being terminated from the journalism brother/sisterhood.

I glance at the dashboard and see that only an hour has gone by—day two is always slower, in perception, than day one when driving. Anticipation and excitement turn into impatience and boredom. Going back to my train of thought, I start to think about the Montana angle. How would sex trafficking work? Montana is close to the Canadian border. The pickings from unsuspecting touring families with young girls are plenty. One would make a mark and develop the right time to nab the victim. Though I wonder how one keeps suspicion away—you can't have a bunch of girls disappear from one spot or else that spot becomes undesirable and no one comes anymore. As Montana is so vast and open, losing tourism would be detrimental to the state. In this day and age of multiple "news" sources on the internet, a person could make up a story about a missing girl—maybe lost on a trail or wandered off with the wrong touring group—to make it look accidental, and even appear to be the parents' fault. It's almost too easy.

Yish. I hate it when I'm required to think like the bad guy. Even though I think I'm being simplistic, in order for me to get to answers, I have to come up with all of the questions. Now I'm wondering if the ring is domestic or if these girls are being shipped out of country. I've gone hiking in small, forested parks—maybe only 3 square miles total—and have been completely turned around, disoriented, and fairly certain I wouldn't be found. Likewise, on any given day, the police flash a photo of a missing girl and most people wouldn't notice her walking right by them. It is easier to become lost or to disappear than people think.

Is it a few people doing this? If so, how would it connect to the

White House, as Eric seems to think? If it is a larger conglomerate, how does it stay so quiet that no one knows or is willing to rat it out? I think one could probably rule out a single terrorist. How the hell does it tie to the White House? What are the parameters for choosing a particular victim? Is it circumstantial or profiled and planned? What kind of money is involved? When the girl is used up, what happens to her? Is she murdered?

How can we have all this technology and this happens? We have technology that can pick up thermal signals in our homes, there is GPS, satellites, drones, and wire taps. How the hell are these human traffickers getting around this? We could embed a chip into every citizen, as we do our pets, but we would be sacrificing personal freedom, a value Americans hold too dear to be willing to depart from it. We are not a risk-adverse society. But where do we draw the line in defense of our most valuable citizens—our children? Kids should have some freedom and opportunities to learn to be grown-up. Maybe the fear of this kind of heartache is what kept me from wanting children of my own.

Sunlight of the new day glistens the corners of my windshield from where I missed scraping off the frost this morning. I shake my head, hoping to snap out of this sad session of thoughts. My playlist is starting to repeat, indicating another 90 minutes have passed. The pressure on my bladder tells me to start looking for a rest stop. I'm halfway to Billings, and while I'd rather stop there, I won't make it. The next exit is 3 miles away, which won't be an issue. I swear I'm going to enjoy the view for the rest of the way and push these dark thoughts away.

Five hours later, I pull into the hotel parking lot, tired but exhilarated by the amazing landscape. There's a reason this place is called "Big Sky Country." It reminded me of the Dixie Chicks song "Wide Open Spaces"; they had to have been envisioning what I saw today: vast snow-capped mountains and endless plains with the occasional midnight blue lake mirroring the mountains. It was cloudless and quiet.

On the interstate, cars approached at irregular intervals. I was startled when I saw an out-of-nowhere flicker of black horns—mountain goats vertically upscaling the steep cliffs. But best of all was watching a majestic moose drinking from one of the lakes. I pulled over and watched him for a while. I knew that he knew I was there, yet he wasn't intimidated in the least by my presence. Why would a 1,500-pound, almost 7-foot creature be afraid of me? The next almost equally intriguing event was when my car ran parallel to a group of at least twenty wolves hovering over what I presumed was a group kill. They were enjoying their meal together, in harmony, again, not concerned about my existence. I wasn't supposed to bring a camera, but honestly, I wasn't going to make a trip here without one. I'm so glad I did. I park and climb out of the Jeep, stretching my back and inhaling the crisp air. This place is like another planet compared to the steel and glass milieu that I call home.

I take a moment to appreciate that the corporations that have somehow squeezed themselves into this land understand that they have to conform to their surroundings and not the other way around. I see my Super 8 motel looks like a lodge with a faux log exterior. The McDonald's a couple of buildings down the street has surrendered its familiar golden arches for a sign bearing its name on top of the building and a totem pole by the entrance. There is little neon that I can see, except for the "Open" sign in a few shops.

While Gardiner is one gateway into Yellowstone, and surely created for the purpose of tourism, it keeps itself humble by not having flash. I almost think it's a ruse of marketing. Perhaps Gardiner keeps itself simple to fool city folk into thinking they're "roughing it." I laugh when I look at all the rented Land Rovers and Jeeps. There isn't a road in Yellowstone where tourists need to be concerned about the terrain. But when all one knows is a concrete jungle, open plains and big rocks can be intimidating. I'll bet the souvenir shops make money hand over fist on "specially" filtered water bottles and overpriced backpacks with a Yellowstone logo. I tell myself to stop being snarky and go to the lobby and check in.

"Welcome to Gardiner," the beautiful, young clerk says pleasantly. She has snow white skin, slightly slanted eyes, and shiny, long, black hair.

"Thank you, Alena," I reply, reading her name tag as I simultaneously pull out my wallet with my driver's license and credit card bearing my new name.

"Ms. Howard, I see you are staying with us for two weeks, is that correct?"

"Yes, I'm looking for a place to rent. A friend has put me in touch with a real estate agent, and I plan to start looking for a place tomorrow."

Alena smiles politely. "How nice you wish to make Gardiner your home."

I smile. I know most of the young people feel somewhat trapped—sick of staying but scared to move out to the big city. A fear of being isolated from the culture has a stronger pull than freedom.

"One can be any age and choose a different life," I offer candidly, looking into her eyes. Her face lights up, ever so slightly, then immediately changes back to the all-business friendly hostess.

"If you would like a larger coffee pot, I can get one for your room for an additional $10, which would include filters. You would have to purchase your own ground coffee, but there is a wonderful roaster in town."

"How do you know me?" I ask with teasing amusement.

"I just sensed it," she volleys back. Then she continues, "We also offer breakfast in the Lodge Room, off to the left, from five to nine a.m. On the first floor there is a laundromat, which is open twenty-four hours a day."

I thank her and complete the transaction. I discover, happily, I'm on the third floor, tucked into a corner away from the elevators. I move the Jeep closer to the corner entrance and grab my stuff. The room is clean, and there is a cubic refrigerator, a queen bed, a dresser, and a nice TV. There's nothing fancy about the bathroom, but it's pristine, and that is all that matters. I decide I should call Eric even though I'd prefer to wait until I'm unpacked, but it will appease his somewhat controlling temperament.

"Hello, Anne, you made wonderful time."

"It's pretty easy to do on these Montana highways—no worries about getting pulled over for going 85."

He laughed lightly. "Glad the trip is done, Miss Leadfoot." He then swiftly changed to business mode. "Are you ready to talk about a plan?"

I sat on the bed with my legs propped, a pen and a pad of hotel paper in hand. "A beginning of a plan anyway. I'm going to need to eat soon."

"Of course. In fact, you could kill two birds with one stone. The restaurant is about two blocks down. This is the target of our venture. My connection, Sonya, is working there as an assistant manager. She's the one who initially tipped me off—she's mad enough to get the ball rolling but is very hesitant to be more involved than that. She knows you're coming and is going to give you a job waiting tables. I'd like you to go there to give the impression you're filling out an application. Enjoy some dinner and ask for Sonya—she'll be there."

"No rest for the weary, I guess. I don't suppose there's an option to move this to tomorrow, is there?"

"Not really. We have a lot of work to do in a short time, and I don't want to lose our chance."

I catch that he keeps saying "we" and "our."

"Eric, I'd like to ask something. You seem invested in this. The pronouns you use are inclusive. What is your get in all of this?"

He pauses for a few seconds, "I want justice, like you do. I also feel responsible for any risks you are about to take. And I say this delicately, I also feel responsible for some of the success you have achieved."

The unease returns. Like the police, I cannot allow people to become entrapped in the drama. I can't let them project their fantasies on my reality. But he does have a point—if not for him, I would not have had the chunk of leads I've received.

I play it cool. "Gotcha. I need an hour to unwind, clean up, and then I'll truck on over there. I just ask for Sonya, right?"

"Yes, I'll let her know you're coming. When you return, please call again, as I'll have a little more information to go over with you."

"Will do."

Click.

———

About an hour later, I make my way to the restaurant with just a small purse containing the phone, a lipstick, my wallet, and the room key. There are about twenty cars parked in the lot, making it look almost full. The entrance has thick double doors, probably made of oak, stained with a deep brown to match the rest of the building.

There is a couple ahead of me, and after the hostess seats them, she turns to me, "Good evening and welcome. How many in your party tonight?"

"Just one. Can you please point out Sonya to me?"

"Follow me," she says. As we enter the main dining room, she points to a 50ish-year-old woman with long, silver hair, black pants, and a dusty purple blouse.

"That's Sonya," she whispers, as she shows me to the booth and hands me a menu. "Do you want me to get her?"

"Not yet, thank you. I'll eat dinner first and then bug her."

The formula for any restaurant pandering to tourists is to offer something they know but given a name that is homogenous to the area. "Yellowstone Chops," "Montana Man-Steak," and "Coyote

Chicken" pop out on the menu. The prices are tourist prices, so I imagine not many of the local working class dine here regularly.

The server brings the glass of chardonnay I ordered and takes my order with a genuine smile on his face. He looks like a transplant, maybe from the West Coast. My estimate is only based on his dialect, his mannerisms—crisp, friendly but not Midwestern bubbly—and his almost metrosexual grooming.

As I wait for dinner, it hits me that it's almost been seventy-two hours since I last spoke to and saw John. It feels surreal, as if I'm gradually becoming Anne Howard and losing being Mara Finegan. I shake the uneasy feeling away and start to observe the other patrons.

One couple, in their thirties, is truly enjoying each other's company, as I see the woman laugh at something the man said. There is a family of five at a half-moon booth that is loud but in that happy-to-be-on-vacation loud. I also see a table of four men in their upper 20s, who are planning the next day's adventure.

Jason, my server, brings me a cup of wild mushroom soup and refills my water. "The hostess told me you were looking to speak to Sonya. Would you like me to get her? She's free for the moment."

"Only if it's not an inconvenience," I reply.

"Not a problem."

A few minutes later, after I've finished my soup, Sonya appears at the table. "Good evening. I understand you are looking for me?" she asks politely.

I motion for her to sit and I tell her I'm a friend of Eric's. She stiffens a bit but remains polite. "Yes, Eric mentioned you'd be here tonight. Please understand, I'll get you the job, but other than that, I don't want any involvement in Eric's plans."

I see a bit of fear in her eyes. "Is there something I should know?"

"Not at all. Eric just makes things . . . complicated at times," she replies too brightly.

"You have my word," I tell her. "Tonight, I'm just observing and seeing if I can pick up any vibes. I'll give you my phone number and if there is a particular person I should be concerned about, would you please call or text me? I would appreciate it."

Sonya hesitated for a moment, then put on a tight smile. "Ms. Howard, it's been wonderful meeting you. Let's have you start the day after tomorrow." She offers her hand for me to shake, which I do, and then she rises to leave as I quickly scribble the phone number on a scratch piece of paper and hand it to her. She takes it, slides it into her pocket, and says, "We'll see you then, enjoy your dinner."

I splurge on a second glass of wine as my dessert after what was a perfect steak. The last two days catch up with me, and I suddenly feel very sleepy. I decide to skip coffee, and after Jason has returned with my receipt and credit card, I head back to the hotel. It's an effort to perform my going-to-bed rituals, and when I turn out the light, I instantly fall asleep.

———

After what seems like only a few minutes, I wake up. The phone says it is 1:32 a.m. I have a headache as a result of the wine and probably not enough water. As I'm now wide awake, I grab my notebook and pen and crawl back into bed. I haven't had time to outline my approach on this. I'm reluctant to share everything with Eric, but I'll have to give him something during our next conversation.

I jot down the details I can recall of the restaurant, sketching a floor plan. Without having seen the kitchen, I cannot possibly know all the exits or if there is a basement or even a separate office. I try to recall the various staff members and anything distinctive, such as how many men, women, their ages, and ethnicity. Then I pull out my laptop and Google a map of Gardiner, committing to memory the different roads in and out of town.

I spend time researching bus and train schedules. There is a small airfield for two-seaters and helicopters just south of Yellowstone. Peeking at the clock, I see that two hours have passed, and even though my mind is churning with ideas on how to smuggle girls in and out of town, I realize I need to sleep more or I'll be useless. I turn out the light and, surprisingly, sleep comes instantly.

———

I can't believe a week has passed and I'm no closer to finding any evidence of any kind of smuggling, prostitution, sex rings—absolutely nothing. A chunk of time has been spent learning my new "job" as a server. Waiting tables is like riding a bike—most aspects of it haven't changed. The computerized ordering system is more sophisticated, yet simpler to learn than what I remember from my college days. Marketing has taken over the restaurant industry. The logos and menu designs are simple and inviting, and it appears only Thesaurus masters are in charge of naming and describing entrees.

I actually enjoy myself, and at times, I forget my real purpose.

But chattering with the patrons aids me in assessment. Over the years, my observation skills have become keener. I do feel a little snarky as I mentally ridicule some of the people who come here for their "wilderness" experience. As I have vacationed in Montana and the Northwest many times, I can pick out the wannabies from a mile away. They all wear the expensive outfits—designer goose down vest and cashmere-lined yoga pants and hats for the women and khakis with lots of cargo pockets, stiff, unscuffed hiking boots, and $400 wind shirts for the men.

Zeroing in on body language, micro-expressions, how people eat, how they discourse with their meal mates, and so much more, I silently profile each person into two groups in my mind: not likely and very possible. But, even the most innocent-looking people can be bloodthirsty serial killers or rapists. If the organization is Eastern European or Middle Eastern, both notorious for sex-trafficking, it would be stupid to have the front men be from those countries as out here in Montana they would stick out like a sore thumb.

In my research, I found that there are quite a few women who run these groups too. A perverted madam, I guess. How does a woman get involved in the trafficking of young girls? One would think some sort of primal instinct wouldn't allow that to happen, right? Sadly, there are many young girls who have been molested by women, but reporting it is even lower than men reporting molestation by women, which also happens. The men don't report it because of the implication that they weren't "man enough" to fight off the abuse. The women don't report it because it is too hard for society to believe that a woman would betray another female in that way.

I did a story on that, which physically made me sick. I didn't want to believe it either. A friend in the district attorney's office had come across sensitive information about a woman who had been fostering children for more than fifteen years. One of the fostered girls, Alissa, had come forward as an adult to share her story of abuse. Something in her just broke, and like a dam, she poured out this story. With Alissa's strength and inner need to fight back, we worked for months to locate her foster brothers and sisters, and to help them confide in us about their own dark experiences. In all, 22 children— girls and boys—had been molested by this woman who was supposed to care and nurture them. Twenty-two children in fifteen years. While it was past the statute of limitations to press charges for those victims, they were able to put that monster away, because detectives and attorneys were able to prove ongoing abuse for the three children she was currently caring for in her home. That bitch is locked up, but only for seven years.

Think of the psychological harm rape and molestation causes and multiply that tenfold for the girls who are trafficked. Not only are they messed up for having any sexual relations, but the ability to form healthy bonds with women, as friends or coworkers, is deeply stagnated. I can't even imagine the healing that would have to happen for these girls to not be scared for having their own children. Many times, these girls grow up thinking they could be abusers too, and they don't have children to avoid the potential demon. I wish every abused girl could meet Alissa—she has two girls and a boy, and a husband who is supportive and helps with Alissa's free speaking engagements. I have never met a stronger woman.

I glance at my notes. Of the people I have put in my "potential" category, there are only two men. I got their names from the credit card slips and asked questions as part of the server banter. I'd ask "Where are you staying?" or "Here for guy bonding or family vacation?" and their body language would determine if I should dig deeper—did they stiffen up, did they look at me suspiciously, those kinds of things.

After hours, I did a little poking at the hotels they stayed at, checked out the rental car companies, and looked for them in different databases. But I didn't come up with anything that would tip them off as real traffickers. Back to the drawing board.

John

It has been two weeks and I'm starting to understand the helplessness and canned worry the World War II mothers, wives, and girlfriends felt. It is astonishing they could go for weeks on end without any connectivity. Since this started, there has been a knot of unease in my gut, and with each day, the knot gets tighter.

Working seems to be the only way I can distract myself. Normally, when I'm immersed in a project, I don't think about Mara during the day. I'm trying to pretend that each day is like every other. Then night comes.

I've never been a guy who goes to the bar after work, and I'm not very social. We hang out with Sean and his wife Erin, Mallory and Jay, Ed and Lorraine, and Emile and Victoria for dinners out or a concert or for a barbeque at someone's house. But of those couples, we are the only ones without children. It's getting harder to do grown-up things with them outside of the home. I have nothing against children, I like kids, but I never had a strong urge for my own. I admit, it's kind of strange for a guy who comes from a big family.

I was surprised that Mara didn't have a burning desire to have kids. Even though she says she doesn't have a nurturing gene, I think she would've been a pretty great mom. I'm not disappointed, I'm not wistful, and I do get my fill with nieces and nephews, playing the awesome uncle. Our life is whole and completely satisfying as it is. I wouldn't change a thing.

Which brings me back to Mara. I have not nor will I ever understand her capacity to absorb the ugliness in the world. Mara's talents as a journalist expose this ugliness in a digestible way. She collects the terrible realities and skillfully regurgitates and reshapes those facts. She pulls people in with her words and incites a collective desire for justice.

Unfortunately, she also has the mindset that evil will not reach her, physically, nor take any part of her soul. It isn't that she doesn't get fearful or believes she is invincible, but I honestly think she thinks she can will harm away.

I guess I'm more of a realist or a pessimist. I'm grateful every time she gets through a tough assignment, but because a person can't be lucky 100 percent of the time, I am also frightened—what thing will happen that ends her roll of luck? She cannot possibly continue without eventually becoming scathed. Yet, more than dying, if she got out now, she would probably be crushed. If I asked her to quit, she would, but the price would be too much for us. Her wings would be clipped and she'd resent me for the rest of our lives.

Yet here we are. This is absolutely the longest we have been apart without any communication. I am tempted every night to call her boss, but then I remember that he doesn't know anything either. I've received a couple of calls from her parents, and I have put on the face of assurance while the knot pulls on my insides. No one knows where she is except this source of hers, Aaron or Eric, or whatever his name is.

Damnit, how can I be so stupid? I'm mad at myself and at Mara for letting her talk me into this. Who would ever just let this happen? Even the freaking Navy Seals have at least a commander who knows where they are.

Okay, John, pull it together. It's a beautiful Saturday morning. Plan the day; keep it filled. I'll go for a run, take a long hot shower, do a little work, call and invite myself over to hang with one of the sibs—make it a good day. I can do this.

I think I'll do a Lake Harriet run, which is a good seven miles from here. At this time of day, there is a smattering of runners, fewer baby strollers, but more bikers. I always find the rivalry between runners and bikers amusing; like the Vikings and the Packers, they have a healthy and respectful dislike. Bikers are just arrogant and rude, in my opinion and experience. They're okay at places like Lake Harriet, where one part of the path is strictly for bikers and one side is for runners, but God Almighty, on actual roads, they are just asses. They want the same rights as car drivers but won't follow the rules, like fully stopping at an intersection. I hate their prissy outfits too.

I set my timer, start my run, then decide to turn the timer off. Today, I just want a run to burn off stress and clear my mind, not to compete. From time to time, this sort of run does me good—the rhythm, the beat of my feet against concrete, the smells of dirt and water, the warmth from head to toe, and the taste of salt from drops of sweat. Emptying my mind, embracing my environment, this is my amphetamine. Looking at my watch, I see I'm already twenty minutes into it. I'm feeling good. I start to see more people—some are focused and some are using the walk or run as a social event.

Coming around a bend in the path, I see a black jeep. For no plausible reason my sides cramp up and my heart begins racing. I make it to the nearest garbage can just as the knot explodes and I puke my guts out.

Mara

Supposedly, the real estate agent friend of Eric's, Matthew, has the rental I'm to use for the rest of my stay here, ready to go. There was a two-day delay because the owner had a plumbing issue to fix. Matthew said he'd swing by and have me follow him around one p.m. It works out since I am not scheduled to be at the restaurant for either the lunch or dinner shift, today or tomorrow.

I have an hour to get stuff packed and checked out, which should only take me another ten to fifteen minutes, as I already have it mostly together. The hotel was understanding about the abnormal checkout time—Eric must have paid them a little extra.

Since sleep sucked again last night, I set the phone timer for twenty minutes so I can take a power nap. It's strange how I always feel better after a power nap versus sleeping for a couple of hours. It usually takes a minute to relax all of my muscles and just let my thoughts wander.

Of course, I start thinking about John. I can only imagine he's going completely nuts. Frankly, so am I. There have been a few more potential leads, but they also all fizzled out. During a call with Eric a few days ago, I brought this up, saying that I'm beginning to doubt anything was going on at all, and that if something didn't start shaking soon, I was out of here. Two weeks in a mediocre hotel, not having communication with John or anyone else is wearing on me.

Eric asked me to give it two more weeks and then told me about the rental house. It was fully furnished, had a nice bed and a newly remodeled bathroom with all the bells and whistles—like six jet sprays in the shower. I can be persuaded when a luxury shower is beckoning to me.

I do feel a little weird about what to do with the tips I've made so far at the restaurant. Surprisingly, I haven't completely lost my touch and have made some bank, which makes me chuckle. Maybe when this assignment is done, I'll give it to the servers at the restaurant. All of them have been very sweet and helpful, and all of them are at least ten years younger. When making small talk, it has been challenging not to screw up on details about me, so I try to keep it vague. Maybe I'll donate the money to a charity working to end sex-trafficking.

The beeper goes off on the alarm, though it feels like I just shut my eyes. I get up anyway and finish packing. By the time I have reconciled with the hotel, I see Matthew waving at me from his

Range Rover. After greeting him and loading my jeep, we get on the road.

We drive on Main Street for a few minutes, and then turn off and head northeast toward a different section of Yellowstone. Twenty minutes later, Matthew turns into the driveway of a rambler that is plain but well-kept. At least it is quieter and more pleasant than another night of listening to traffic go by until midnight.

Matthew offers to take my suitcase, leaving me with the rest. I stop and turn around to see the view. We are at a higher elevation, so I can see the mountains clearly. I can also see Main Street lined with cars the size of ants. I'll have to make sure I give myself at least thirty to forty minutes to get to the restaurant, I mentally note. The view is outstanding. Definitely not the worst place I've been holed up for during an assignment.

Matthew holds the door for me, and we step immediately into a small, quaint, but kitschy living room. There is a love seat, a recliner, and a nice TV surrounded by four lemon yellow walls.

"This is cool. Way better than the hotel," I say to Matthew.

"Eric does try to be accommodating," he replies.

I head to the galley-style kitchen, its walls painted sky blue with a moose stencil bordering the top. There is a basic refrigerator, an older gas oven, and a two-seater table and chairs. I venture into the hallway and find a queen-sized bed in a lilac bedroom. Next to it, I peek into the white bathroom with gray highlights. Not sure what definition they used for remodeling, as it is rather dull—maybe the shower itself is the only thing remodeled. But I'm not complaining—it is very clean and it isn't a hotel.

"I'll call Eric later and thank him for doing this."

"You can thank him now, if you'd like," he says.

I'm confused by both his comment and his tone. He casts a creepy smile as a second man sidesteps from behind Matthew and into my view.

"Hello, Mara."

Mara

The voice is somewhat familiar, as is the face. In my confusion, I'm having trouble placing them both. But Matthew just said . . .

"Eric?"

The man stepped in closer, and again, recognition was coming clearer. "Today you know me as Eric. If you try a little harder, perhaps my real identity will become apparent."

"I'm sorry, Eric, I'm usually pretty good with faces, but I'm drawing a blank."

The small inner voice that has always guided me is stirring, and acid creeps up my throat. Danger alarms are going off in my body with each passing moment, but I'm transfixed by what is unraveling.

Eric continued, "I, too, have an Irish name. I was raised in the same town as you. I am only slightly older than you are."

My face must not have registered any recall because his eyes turn dark, his smile morphs into a sneer, and his voice fills with venom. "Think, Mara. Whose heart did you break so many years ago? I know you've had a few men in your life, so maybe that didn't help. But did you make a lifetime commitment to anyone but me? Did you ruin any more lives besides mine, did you disrupt other great dreams? C'mon Mara, think hard," he jeered.

I started to retort that John is the only man I had ever committed to, but then it clicked. My disbelief so engulfing, I couldn't think straight. "Todd?" I ask quietly.

"Ladies and gentlemen, she wins the prize! Matthew, are you amazed at how smart our girl is? Not me, I always knew she was brilliant—in some things, anyway."

"Why, Todd? Why this charade of being my informant all these years? Why not just be you and not all this cloak-and-dagger stuff?" I ask with a hint of anger.

"I think I spoke too soon, Matthew. Let's continue the game and see if our bright girl figures it out," he says sarcastically.

"Okay, Todd, or Eric, or whoever. We went out in high school and we broke up and moved on with our lives. Or at least I did. What the hell have you been doing? Have you been spying on me since then? That's both pathetic and creepy." Now I was starting to get pissed, but I continue, "You didn't like that I didn't plan on being a servant wife and join you in your cultish notions, which by the way, never quite matched up with what I have always believed

God to be about."

"Temper, temper, Mara. You always did have a short fuse. You really should work on that."

"And you should get a life," I say harshly. "Are you really trying to do good by helping me? Do you think we have a bond now because of that? If you wanted to be a partner, you could've reached out and asked. It's been over twenty years! Bygones are bygones. I would've considered working with you outright, but you went way past the line with this ridiculous game. What was the point of all the secrecy?" I was a mix of confusion, anger, and disbelief over this discovery.

"Your partner? Ha! That's rich, Mara. You would still be writing fluff pieces without me. I am the reason you have what you have. And yet, you have so little gratitude."

"Oh please. As if you are my only informant. Do you need gratitude? Okay, thank you for your clues and assistance over the years. Is that what you want to hear? Thank you sooooooooo much," I say with a smirk.

"Step cautiously, Mara."

"And by the way, maybe your luck has run out, as this whole trafficking thing has turned up absolutely nothing. It's been a waste of time, except that it was great to come out to Montana again."

"You know, Mara, it was a bit insulting when your parents didn't invite me to enjoy a family vacation. My family was always so good to you," he replies wistfully.

"Seriously? You're hung up about that? Was there ever really a story? Did you just want a little reunion in Montana?" I ask.

"That's one way to look at it," he says with a smile toward Matthew.

"Fabulous. Thanks again for the vacation. I'll write you a check to reimburse you for all of the expenses, as I sure as hell don't want to owe you for anything." I went to the bedroom to get my suitcase and computer bag, came back to the living room with the Jeep keys, and headed for the door. Matthew blocked my path.

"Get. Out. Of. My. Way," I snarl to the man I thought was a nice guy.

"Your sharp brain isn't connecting the dots, Mara," Todd says behind me.

I spin around. "Tell your buddy to move it. I'm going home. Here's the damn keys, I'll fucking walk down this fucking hill, but I'm leaving." As the last words come out, I swing my computer bag at Matthew, clocking him in the face, hoping to bust his nose. I rush out and start running, abandoning my suitcase but keeping the computer bag, as I heard the howls of pain I inflicted.

I run hard, slipping frequently on the gravel and almost twisting my ankle, adrenaline pushing me forward. I hear a door slam, and I duck behind a rock that was too small to conceal me.

"Mara," I hear Todd announce, "I've planned too long for this silliness to continue."

My brain quickly assesses my options. I could bolt in the hopes that I could outrun them and get to the bottom before they could catch me. Or I could stay still, hope they pass me by, and then turn a different direction, if there was one. I decide to take my chances. I calm myself enough to regulate my breathing, get my head in order, and prepare my body to push itself as fast as possible. Silently, I count to three and then bolt. I half run, half slide down the gravel road, not sure if I'm being followed, but I wasn't going to look behind me. The weight of the computer bag slung around my neck and chest is constantly bruising my side, but I feel nothing but the tinny taste of fear and determination coating my throat. About two hundred yards out, I estimate, is the smooth concrete road, heading back to Main Street. If I can make it to town, I have a fighting chance.

My lungs hurt from the thinness of the higher altitude and my bum knee burns with pain, but getting caught is not an option. Too many news stories' odds indicated my getting caught would not be in my favor. Just as I was about to hit pavement, the black Jeep screeched in front of me.

"How the hell . . ."

A very angry Todd burst out of the Jeep, pressing one hand over my mouth while wrapping my left arm behind my back. Terrified, I fling my head back as hard as I could and feel it connect squarely to the bridge of his nose. Simultaneously, I dig my heel into the side of his knee. As his grip releases, I take off down the road—I couldn't go off the road as the slope is too steep and there are too many jagged rocks.

Two steps away, I'm blindsided—tackled from the left by Matthew. My head hits the pavement, and I start feeling woozy. Matthew yanks me up by my hair and pulls me into the Jeep; my arms flailing but hitting only air. Then a rag is pressed hard against my nose and mouth, Todd's bloody but smiling face over mine, and then all goes black.

My eyelids flutter as I try to move, a wall of gray fog in front of them. A dull throb pounds across my eyebrows and the bridge of my nose. I try shaking off the fog and realize I cannot move my legs and arms. I open my eyes wide enough, and after finally being able to focus, I see that I'm bound to one of the kitchen chairs.

I look around and don't see Todd or Matthew. I know if I struggle against the rope it will only grate on my wrists and make the skin raw and bloody, which will make it sticky and harder to get my hands out. I start conjuring saliva; as gross as it seems, if I can get the rope moist, it might be easier to loosen the knots. I primarily work on my right hand, alternating spitting on it and trying to bend over far enough so I can use my teeth to try to tug on the rope, carefully aiming for the side that will loosen rather than tighten. I'm trying not to let fear or anger quicken my pulse, as I don't want to risk overexertion and possibly passing out. After a few minutes, it feels like I'm making some headway, but then I hear voices and I try to go faster.

"Matthew, come see. Our Mara has woken up," Todd says as he enters the kitchen. "I must have missed where you took defense training, shame on me, but I am impressed. Matthew on the other hand . . ." he nods in acknowledgement to Matthew, as he too enters the kitchen, with a bandage over his nose, ". . . is not as impressed as he is furious. I think you broke his nose."

I sneer, "I'd be happy to break anything else if you would loosen the ropes."

Todd's face remains placid. "You did split my lip. I am fortunate not to have chipped or lost a tooth."

"Happy to oblige."

Todd pulls one of the other kitchen chairs in front of me, straddling it, arms across the top, as if we are going to have a heart-to-heart chat. "Mara, I am sure your insatiable curiosity has thousands of questions," he says calmly, as my eyes burn into his. "I'm just going to lay things out here for you. Shortly after you thought it wise to end our relationship, I was completely heartbroken. I couldn't understand, having been obedient to God, understanding you were chosen for me by Him, that He would take you away."

"God has positively nothing in common with you, you sad, delusional fuck," I say viciously.

He grabs my face, pinching the fleshy but hollow space just below the cheekbone. "Be very careful, Mara. You know nothing about

God, and you will not use such grotesque language."

We stare hard at each other for a few more seconds and then he releases his grip on my face. I now know a couple of ways to agitate him—if I can distract by taunting him, I can keep trying to loosen the ropes.

"After a few months, unable to be consoled, I understood that I was weak, that God was showing me you for the future. I had to develop my mental skills, learn to become a more righteous man. I had to first dedicate myself to focusing on learning the intelligence industry, specifically through technology and how to artistically unleash its powers. It is how I have amassed a nice fortune and have the ability to prepare properly."

"Prepare for what? I don't think most men of the cloth are ordained hackers," I reply with rancor.

Todd leans back a little, and with a too cool smile he looks back over at Matthew, who smiles back at him. Then, he looks back at me and says, "Holy indemnification."

There is still a bit of gray floating in my brain, but then it hits me. "You think kidnapping me is some God-sanctioned action?" I ask incredulously. "What does this accomplish? You want me to wear your class ring or something? This is beyond absurd."

He shakes his head, looks down at the floor. "No, dear one, you're not even close. You're thinking too small. You were supposed to be my mate for life. I thought God started that in high school, but I was wrong. I was to wait until you were grown-up. Unfortunately, you were so blinded by ambition that you didn't see God's vision for you. You were to be my wife and bear my children. But you ruined everything by allowing yourself to fall to the carnal secular life. How could you bear standing in a church, no less, and take holy vows of marriage to a heathen like John? You are simply untouchable to me now. I've bore this burden, this heaviness that we cannot be joined together as God intended."

My eyes must have been bulging. "Seriously? A high school romance didn't pan out and so now you're kidnapping me? If I'm so untouchable, why am I here? What purpose does this serve, and how do you know John?" I'm hoping that he is offended enough by my "secular" life that he won't do me any bodily harm, that it wouldn't fit this sociopath's modus operandi.

He must have read my thoughts, "Don't worry, Mara, I am beyond sexual gratification—it is a pathetic need for pathetic people. Besides, you are a filthy whore, I mean goodness, how many men have you slept with over the years?"

He is truly, truly nuts. "None of your fucking business," I reply snottily and once again he grabs my face. "You will stop. I will not have you be disrespectful." He lets go and starts pacing, collecting himself.

"You aren't going to rape me, so what do you want?" I ask evenly.

"As I said, indemnification. Some would call it revenge, perhaps. I see it as God's judgment on you."

I laugh. "Because God has nothing better to do then avenge a homely nerd for a high school thing. How arrogant is that? You think God works that way? That He would ordain a kidnapping? You are simply insane, and I really do pity you." I could tell I was pissing him off, which would work in my favor, psychologically, or so I reason, as I keep trying to loosen the knots.

Todd moves into the living room. I see him pacing. Matthew never takes his eyes off me. "What are you staring at, you freaking goon?" He says nothing but has an all-knowing look on his face. "What do you gain from this, Matthew? You understand that now you're tied to this; you too will be in prison for the rest of your life? Is it money? I can get money. Why not help me escape and free yourself from this lunatic?"

He continues to say nothing.

"Funny you should talk about imprisonment, Mara," Todd says as he walks back into the kitchen.

"The two of you will not keep me here forever. I will get out of here," I reply defiantly.

He then holds a picture of John in front of me. On the bottom, right-hand corner is Saturday's date. It shows John walking from his car to the front door of his office. There's no denying it was him.

Eyes narrowed, I say, "You could have manipulated the date on the picture and taken that anytime."

"That is true. But I want you to focus hard on the next picture."

He pulls out another photo that shows a newspaper on John's desk with yesterday's date on it. Yesterday was Monday. For the first time since this crazy thing began, fear starts to overtake anger.

"How the hell did you get into John's office? They have a fairly elaborate alarm system."

"Please, that was child's play. I could walk into the Pentagon if I really wanted to," he responds condescendingly.

I let my fury come back. "What do you want with John? He hasn't done anything to you; leave him out of this."

"Mara, Mara, he is the focus of all of this. I have been waiting, planning, and savoring this for a long time, but I see that your impatience is getting the worst of you." He sighed. "I think I need to lay this out for you before you wear yourself out trying to get out of the ropes."

The flurry of emotions renders me silent. My head is darting, trying to think of all the different things Todd intends to do to John. I'm sick thinking that any harm is to come to him. I realize he could be killed, or maybe, I think, with cold gripping my heart, he's already dead.

"Here are the rules of the game, Mara. As long as you stay here, peacefully carving out your new life in Montana, John remains safe. As long as you do not try to communicate with him, John remains safe. As long you do not communicate with anyone outside of this place, John remains safe. This includes contact with the police, news agencies, Facebook, relatives, or anyone else who knows you as Mara. This is your new home. You have a job waiting tables, you have the serenity of the mountains, I even have a very expensive mountain bike in the garage for your pleasure. I'm sure you'll make friends and enjoy a comfortable existence."

"For how long?"

Todd laughs a deep, long bellyache laugh. He wipes a tear from the corner of his eye while resting his other hand on Matthew's shoulder. "Did you hear her? She still is quite amusing. Oh, my goodness, this is even better than I envisioned. I wanted a little fear, knew there'd be the fiery temper, but this naivete, I didn't imagine!"

He took a few minutes to still the laughter, then walks up to me, his thumb tilting my chin upward, and says in his sweetest voice, "For the rest of your life."

And as he walks out of the room, still laughing, I start screaming.

Part 3

Six Months Later—Mara

It has been about six months since this nightmare began. In so many ways I'm broken, yet I'm resolved to do whatever it takes to keep John alive. There are even more rules to follow now than in the beginning. I have been incapable of outwitting this perverse maniac. I have a computer, but my captor is a tech whiz, so every stroke of the keyboard could be recorded. Obviously, Facebook or any other social media is out of the question.

I can't contact our friends, my family, or my editor Ron. Todd knows who they are, and I have to assume he has the means to hack any accounts they may have. Clearly, the authorities are not the answer. I know this house is watched, but I went over every inch of the house for anything that resembles a bug or a camera and cautiously concluded the inside of the house is not filmed. I was left the Jeep, but I know there is tracking device on it that I'd been warned not to remove.

I can't send a letter or a postcard, as I know John's office and our home is watched. I don't even want to try sending a note to my parents for fear they will be harmed.

And then there's the worst part.

Every few weeks, I get a package from an unknown, untraceable place that contains a letter from Todd taunting me in some way and photos of John living his life. A month after my captivity began, I received a video that showed the police, or Todd's goons disguised as police, at our house telling John that I am dead. He was told I died in a crash, swerving on a slick mountain road in Colorado, and that no remains were to be found. As proof, he was given my suitcase with my identity tag on the inside with our address on it, burnt quite severely, along with some strands of my hair that was DNA tested.

The video showed the conversation along with John breaking down. It was horrible, and I'll never be able to erase that from my mind. Seeing John slump against the wall, deflating like a punctured tire. It was as if he aged ten years instantly. I've never seen him hurting so bad, and it tears at me that I'm the cause of it. I only watched it once, and afterward, I cried, tore at my clothes, beat the wall, and then drank heavily.

I now live—if one can call it living—believing I am watched every minute. I know I'm not, but I can't afford to make any mistakes. I still work at the restaurant, which is my only income now, and the days just blend from one to the next. Some days, I feel like I should just make it a reality, that I should just kill myself, but the bastard took that away too.

"If you try to take the easy way out, well, you will never know what will happen to John, will you?" Todd had threatened me.

Some days, I'm angry—angrier than I've ever been in my life. After I bloodied my knuckles against the wall for the third time, I realized that being angry would only satisfy him. At least if I showed it on the outside. Now, I keep it smoldering under the surface, letting my hatred take on the blackest of black.

But I can only keep that up for so long. Some days I cry and am desperately hopeless. I drink now more than I ever did, just to numb the sharpness of this pain. Once in a while, I try to remember the story of Job. God allowed the devil to take everything away from him so he would curse God. While it would be easy to blame God, I just can't. I can still recall all the beauty and good I've experienced and maybe I've now had mine. I had the privilege of being partnered with the best man a woman could ever hope for, better than I thought I deserved. But then I pray and no answers come, and I'm just not as strong as Job.

John

I can't say I would feel "better" if I knew exactly what happened. It is impossible to know, all they said is that she slid on a mountain road and fell off the cliff, that there is no chance she could have survived. If she did survive, she would have found a way to reach someone. She would've hopped on one leg for days on end if she had to—she is that strong and stubborn. What if she did survive and had amnesia and didn't know where to go or who to call, or even remember me, us?

It's been six months and I cannot move forward. I just don't have absolute proof, and I still feel her presence. If she's gone, I wouldn't feel her presence, right? Maybe it's survivor's guilt. Except I can't even have that because I don't know *for sure if she is fucking dead or alive*!

Shit! My damn knuckle must be broken. Fuck! The shards of mirror glass surround me on the floor and in the bathroom sink, red from the dripping blood of my hand. I can see a couple of slight, shiny pieces in the open cut. Damnit! Instead of opening the cabinet door, I just reach through, avoiding the hanging, jagged pieces of mirror for the antiseptic and bandages. How is it that when one feels so desperate the body kicks into self-preservation mode? Why do I care if the cut gets infected? Why do I want to live?

I sit on the toilet seat to better steady myself to clean and wrap my hand. Somehow, this pain numbs the rest of me, and I go into autopilot—cleaning up the mess, grabbing another beer, and blankly setting myself in front of the television. Days like this, it is of no use, trying not to think or remember.

I still think there's a chance that Mara could still be alive, so why doesn't anyone else? Everyone else has accepted it, and they try to politely tell me I might be in denial and that I should go to counseling. There was no body found. There was nothing to indicate foul play, said the detectives on the case. What pieces of the Jeep could be removed from the scene, which was little, didn't show any tampering. The skid marks on the road verified the story.

My friends and family tell me how sorry they are. I believe them, but at the same time, I resent them. They get to go home every night. They get to interact with their spouses, their kids, and their friends. They get bedroom talks, intimacy. They get to be annoyed about toothpaste tubes and rearrange their spouse's attempt at loading the dishwasher. Everyone is uncomfortable around me. I feel their thick, syrupy empathy, and I hate it. Excuse the fuck out of me if they're uncomfortable.

My eyes and nose run simultaneously, dripping unto my sweatshirt—the Notre Dame sweatshirt Mara gave me a few years ago. I can't even bring myself to get rid of her clothing; not while a hint of her scent lingers, not while I still feel the tiniest remnants of hope that she is still alive—it would be a betrayal to give up on her.

I even hired my own detective. A client of Ed Mansfield's, my partner, provided a referral. All I was told was the skidded tire tracks were found in Colorado Springs, and that was approximately three days after the accident. It's a wide berth for one detective to comb through. There are lots of resorts, hotels, or highway dives to tackle. And who knows? Maybe she wasn't staying in a commercial place but in a rented apartment? Joel Crane looked through at least one hundred places, went to hospitals, clinics, and even churches. He went to the local police and talked to the detective who looked into the accident and had sent a report to the local police, who informed me of the news. Nothing.

The local police did not feel there was any vicious attack or even a hit and run. But they were not 100 percent sure what caused the skidding. There wasn't any rain, snow, or ice that day. There were no other skid marks from other cars. Their best explanation was that there must have been faulty breaks or driver error. And while I'll readily admit that Mara had a lead foot, she wasn't reckless—crossing off driver error.

Maybe being with Mara as long as I have has made me more suspicious. I now tend to be a little more open about conspiracy theories, jaded by the cruelty of the outside world I didn't want to believe. I'm sure Mara has pissed off an extensive list of people, but I don't recall any stories she did that would lead to actual threats, let alone murder. I made a list of possible enemies, who really were larger government types, and provided clippings of provocative stories to Joel so he could dig deeper.

And now I don't have the $50,000 cash Mara and I had in our emergency fund, nor do I have any more answers—just crossed out lines of potential. I think Joel did the best he could, and he gave me another week for free. I know he felt bad, but Mara wouldn't want me to beg, though I would if it would make a difference.

Mara's and my parents gave me my space to go down this path, but after three months, the four of them came to me and asked for my blessing to have a memorial service. I was so angry at first. I couldn't believe they had given up so easily.

"How can you all gang up on me like this? Do you want her to be dead so you can move on with your golfing buddies, your art workshops, and your vacations?" I despicably yelled at them.

"John," my mother said, "you aren't the only one feeling loss here. Mara is another daughter to us, and obviously the heart of Bill and Lynne. All of us will be heartbroken for her and for you forever, but her spirit needs peace. She needs to believe you will be okay in her absence."

"Oh, please. Don't give me that crap. Mara will be a haunting, nagging ghost, not some peaceful spirit," I said, trying to be sort of funny while simultaneously being a jackass.

"Mara is gone, John," Bill responded. "Even if she initially survived the fall, was she paralyzed? Did she freeze to death or bleed out? God Almighty, I hope not. I hope it was quick and painless. But you know no one survives this long in the wilderness, even someone with great skill to do so. Lynne and I will support you in any way we can, but we need you to help us too. Help us let our beautiful . . ." he started to struggle with tears, ". . . amazing daughter go to Heaven."

Mara

I had always wondered how someone got brainwashed into a cult or how someone survived being a prisoner of war or survived years of child abuse. The cascade of emotions, ones I had never truly felt before, have washed over me. At first, I was in complete disbelief that this was happening. I was rebellious, ready to fight. When in this mindset, something in your DNA believes the fight will be fair; that it will be fought with barbs and logic. Using scorching, below-the-belt statements, and flinging them acidly, that is normal emotional war and eventually the fight will end. But that was not how this was working. Once I realized that, I got scared as hell.

He smelled the fear and proceeded to take it and use it to increase my submission. I knew from years at the newspaper and watching *NCIS*, that brutality happens. But until it happens to you, you think it unfathomable that it ever could. The fear was so strong, I wanted to succumb to it, to make it go away. I wanted to believe that if I did as I was told, it wouldn't get any worse.

It's a lie. The perpetrator will continue to harm, abuse, and destroy as long as he has the power to do so. There is no incentive to do otherwise. The power over another human being is intoxicating. John would be putty in my hands whenever I dressed up for a party or other formal event, and that was powerful to my ego. A sick narcissist like Todd wants you to screw up so they can unleash their fury, their version of justice. It gets to a point where nothing the victim does is right and thus lives in constant fear, accepting the abuse as something deserved.

His verbal abuse had no effect on me. I was toughened up by my experiences in the dark worlds I investigated. My fear was that once I was reunited with John, he would be too traumatized to take me back. I was scared he would see me as damaged goods. It happens. The spouse or partner thinks the other is so fragile, they will recoil at every touch or flip out with the wrong words said. It becomes too much to see the person they love changed so unrecognizably.

If I just took it passively, Todd would only continue; if I fought it, he'd take it to the next level, and if that meant harm to John, I couldn't let that happen. Being who I am, though, doesn't allow me to not fight—the thought of taking it willingly was completely humiliating, as it was intended to be.

Mara

I reach over to the other side of the bed, expecting him to be there. He sometimes sleeps on his back, but mainly he faces the wall, away from me. He isn't there. Sensory memory is betrayed in thinking the sheets or the pillows will still be warm from the heat of his body. That heat could still be felt even after he had risen to take a shower in the mornings. The warmth and the traces of his scent, a bit of perspiration, mixed with his bodywash, would be traceable.

After several months, I still fall for it. Like the *Peanuts* comic strip where Lucy once again makes Charlie Brown believe she'll hold the football only to pull it away and watch him land hard on his back, I am frustrated and feel like such a fool, with my heart hurting just as much. I'm more terrified of losing what that warmth feels like or forgetting his scent.

Damn alarm. Opening my eyes again, I confirm that it is indeed six-thirty. Though I keep black thermal blinds on my bedroom window, the powerful rays of the sun push through pale light, the rising light of an early mountain morning. There is enough cool dampness to make me tingle with chills as I slowly expose parts of my body from the down comforter. The heavy charcoal comforter is one of the very few luxuries I purchased early in my captivity. Because my bed is my solace, I feel like sludge dragging myself out of it to face yet another day.

I know there are worse places to live. The cold and the isolation from mainstream life are a small price to pay when I get to see mountains every day. I see elk pass through, with their proud rack of antlers, reminding me that I am residing on their land. I hear the occasional howls and calls of wolves and coyotes. Then there is every dawn and sunset, depending on the time of year, each different in their variance of blues, pinks, purples, and oranges. All in all, it's not a bad refuge to seek solitude, relaxation, or in my case, imprisonment.

My Sherpa-lined moccasins are my other had-to-have item in this very small, bland house. I slip my feet in, which gives me the courage to keep to the task of being part of the day. The cheerless bathroom is always my first destination. The shower allows for five to seven minutes of somewhat warm water, with barely more pressure than a garden hose.

The toilet may be the only thing running reliably, though it is ancient, with hard water stains that, for all my attempts, cannot seem to get back to white. The nozzle to the so-called hot water side of the sink's faucet squeaks on and off. The medicine cabinet mirror has a crack in the upper right-hand corner and has just enough room for general amenities and first-aid items. The vanity, I swear, is made of tin with two rusted drawers with faded floral lining in them.

I can live with the sad, shabby decor because I cannot afford to spend precious resources on improving it. I did allow myself to purchase two sets of the plushiest towels I could find in lilac and silvery gray. Aside from my bed, my brief hot showers provide much-needed relief from the stresses of the day and my overall anxiety. Other than those things, I refuse to do anything to the house to make it homier, because I do believe in my heart of hearts, that one day I will get to leave this place and go home. This hope sustains me. I don't know the form or signal or whether I'll recognize my deliverance, but I continue to believe it will come. Until that day appears, I cannot give in to letting my guard down, get sloppy in my actions, or be relaxed enough to fully trust anyone here.

Brushing my teeth and rinsing my face shakes out most of the fog in my head. The absolute most important next step is coffee. People are asked what are the top five things they would need if on a remote island—coffee is on my list. I've been a coffee addict since I was sixteen. Mercifully, there is a roaster here in town that supplies most of the resorts and restaurants. For working a few days a week, the owner, Damon Richards, sells me two pounds of his amazing dark roast for a fraction of the retail price. Taking on a second part-time job filled more of my time. I will do whatever I can to be away from the house—my enlarged prison cell.

I was a little nervous when I had my interview with Damon. One of the things about Montana I love is how everything is blunt and spelled out. At home there are so many names of restaurants and unique retail shops that are obscure. I think retail snobs believe the more mysterious the name, the more enticing it will be. I know many acquaintances who will walk out the door of such a place, spending $90 or more for a pair of regular blue jeans with a few sequins sewed to the back pockets just because the name of the place sounded hip, as opposed to just going to the Gap or Old Navy.

Damon is an optimistic sort with more street smarts than most cops I know. He is gracious with customers and has a disarming smile, but he rarely lets anyone manipulate him. I thought about how I came to the Roastery. I needed to find a part-time job at a place where I could use someone else's computer. As all of Gardiner is small businesses, I had to define some parameters for my search.

The most important being what business is closest to my personality and my life at home. Which means the office of an insurance salesperson wasn't going to fit. After reviewing a few possibilities, I remembered my first night in Gardiner, where the hotel clerk mentioned the town's roaster.

At the restaurant, I had seen five-pound bags of coffee with "The Roastery" labels on them—colorful, fun, and at the bottom "Roasted fresh in Big Sky Country—Home of Yellowstone." It had to be the same place the hotel clerk referenced. During a shift at the restaurant, I casually asked one of my coworkers about it and got a good vibe.

"Damon Richards is a super nice guy. He comes to the restaurant with his family frequently. They moved here from San Francisco, but he has worked hard to be part of the community. He donates money and beans for a variety of charity events and says hi to everyone. Some would say he's too friendly, but those of us who've lived here forever could use a little more friendliness."

I took that as a good sign. After my shift, I walked the mile to his place, went inside, and introduced myself.

"Mr. Richards? Hi, my name is Anne Howard, and I just moved here not too long ago, after my divorce. I work at the steakhouse on Main Street, but I'm looking for another part-time job to supplement the bad tip days."

"Nice to meet you, Ms. Howard, but I'm not really hiring. I am a one-man shop—wish I could help," he said earnestly as he started to turn away to get back to work.

"Mr. Richards . . ."

"Damon, please."

"Damon—I see the two roasters, a bunch of bags all over the place, and no offense, but a couple of bags under your eyes. I'm not looking to get rich, I just need a safe place to do work on my novel. Due to my ex shutting down my access, I can't get into my account. If you could afford me just a couple hours a week to use your computer, with a different profile, I'll work three to four shifts a week for the price of two—and a couple pounds of coffee.

"You can't tell me you can't use the help. And during my shifts at the restaurant, I'll tell my customers about your coffee." I learned telling as much truth under an alias helps plausibility and credibility. Also, I needed to get going on a plan that had been formulating in my mind.

Damon broke into a smile. "That is a most unique proposition. I like your blunt, no BS approach. It's much like the bean farmers I buy from. Aside from providing an income for my family and not being stuck in an office, part of the purpose of this company is to help a group of women in South America. There are eight of them with a total of four acres, trying to survive on their own. Their beans are some of the best I've ever had, and it makes me feel good to help this collective, to help them gain financial independence. It puts me in a good light with my wife too. Okay, Anne, I can't pay much, but yes, I could use your help. What's your novel about?"

To appeal to the information he just gave me, I said the novel was about Kurdish women widowed during the Gulf War. I continued by saying that trying to do research with noisy neighbors or working with the library's unreliable internet was getting frustrating.

"I totally get it. Sometimes I come down here and just smoke a cigar when I need a break from the clan," Damon acknowledged sympathetically. "Are you okay with being paid in cash and beans?" I nodded. "Then if you come back on Tuesday, I'll get a key made. If you can do eight a.m. to eleven a few days a week, Anne, I think we can make this work."

He stood, I stood, and we shook hands. Making up the story was the easy part, acting the part of my new persona was harder. I kept saying my new name in front of the mirror dozens of times. I practiced my new signature several times a day. I wrote up a few scenarios where I might be caught off guard and end up out of character. It was the role of a lifetime—to survive, I had to be perfect.

By all appearances, by all evidence available, Mara Lauren Riley was dead. And dead is what she had to be. My happy life, my friends, my home, and my career, was the price for saving John's life.

———

After spending a couple hours formulating my thoughts the next morning, I had the beginnings of a plan. On Tuesday, I took a quick shower, dressed in my server uniform, and grabbed my backpack, which had a notebook, a sandwich, a bottle of water, and a bag of lemon drops. Deciding the weather was decent enough, I rode my bike to the Roastery, stopping first at the tourist "I need this" store to purchase two flash drives.

I wanted the drives so I could take information I found and hide it in two places. I also wrote any notes in a cryptic language that I created for myself a long time ago. It's shorthand that only I can understand. It's amazing what little things can help in the unknown. I know that before I log out each time, I'll need to copy whatever info I've found onto the drive, then obliterate all my searches to, hopefully, wipe away my cyber footprint. It's the best I can do as a non-techie.

Damon waved hello as I parked my bike in the hallway. He met me as I made my way to the small warehouse space that served as the roasting room and the packaging and shipping space. Damon has a small office with his computer, but then up against one of the walls is a computer on an ancient wooden desk with a beat-up roller office chair. This is where the various labels and shipping documents are printed.

Damon began with the overview of his company. "We only make five different coffees: Gardiner Dark, Mountain Glory, and Apsaaloke Dawn, which is roasted with secret herbs grown by the tribe and known to just me and Chief Aldon Rushing Water. Then there are the two that are just for the Yellowstone park shops and local restaurants and hotels: Moose Mud and Yellowstone Dusk.

"The last two," he continued, "are sold for four dollars more per pound at the hotels and restaurants so they can make a few extra bucks."

Based on the photos and plaques on the wall, Damon had endeared himself to the community. They all show him and his family smiling with what appears to be a group of high school teachers, then the one surrounded by carts of books, and one with him surrounded by a Little League team and one with a girls' softball team.

"Looks like you have embraced the community nicely."

"While I am sincere, it's all about marketing. By being part of events and making donations of time, money, and beans, do you think any of the hotels will brew anything else?" he says with a playful smile.

"And then there's the booth at the annual festival, which happens right before tourist season kicks into gear as a means of getting people psyched up to be happy hosts for the next six months. Nothing like pumping caffeine into fair-frenzied parents."

I couldn't help but laugh. Damon was charming—it would be easy to fall under his spell. He's not bad looking either. I needed to be wary; charming people can also be very dangerous.

"Do your wife or kids help out?"

"Emma, my wife, is the president and CEO of our household. We're one of those crazy couples who have six kids, ages three to thirteen. They're awesome, but homeschooling and activities keeps Emma on the go, and she absolutely loves it."

A small wave of regret passes through me. "I was told you came from San Francisco, what made you leave?"

"I loved it there. Both Emma and I were raised in nearby Sausalito. She was running a substantial nonprofit, and I was a marketing director for a very profitable software company. But I was traveling nonstop, and having three kids in daycare is ridiculously expensive. One night at dinner, we realized we had overscheduled and were going to miss our oldest daughter's first orchestra concert. We decided right then that it was no way to live and not fair to our kids."

I was liking this guy more and more. "That's pretty admirable in this age where materialism and titles have increased in importance."

"It's not that I don't miss it from time to time. And we didn't come here broke by any means. My house sold for $2.5 million and my house here—twice as big, cost $300,000 to build. We are coffee nuts. I had the means to buy the equipment and this building outright. I don't need to pay myself a lot of money as a result. And I get my jollies on making new deals and having clients who love me," he paused. "Geesh, that whole spiel probably sounded arrogant."

"Not at all," I reassured him. "It sounds like good planning."

"My wife and I don't have headaches anymore, we get sleep, our kids are happy in this place. They have space to run and explore, time to ride horses, time to be creative—it's how it should be. Luckily, our oldest, Janie, wasn't in tween years yet when we moved here. We may have just saved ourselves a lot of heartache in that she isn't competing for the most expensive jeans or wearing a shitload of makeup at thirteen."

His commentary makes me remember the joyful vacations here.

"But enough about me, Anne. Where are you from again?"

Quickly, I get my facade in place. "My ex and I lived in Chicago—where we are both from. I never got to go west much, and the divorce was pricey. Living in the steel and concrete world wasn't how I wanted to continue my life, which was part of the reason we divorced. Now that I'm here, I don't want to leave," I lie. I want nothing more than to leave this place—this place that used to represent happiness is now a prison.

"What did you do in Chicago?"

"A few things. I was an English tutor, I wrote copy for an advertising agency, technical copy for a few tech firms, all as a consultant. My husband was a high-powered attorney. When we got married, we planned on having kids, and then it just wasn't ever the right time, as he was always working to keep his billables up, too exhausted to put effort into us. Eventually, we lost our window of opportunity and lost ourselves."

I may have laid it on a little too thick, but it must have been believable, as he had a look of pity on his face. "Don't worry, I'm fine. Better than I've ever been, in fact. And now everything I do is on my terms. I just don't have a million events to go to anymore— which is fine with me. While I didn't fight for the house, I did get a nice payoff. I asked for one chunk instead of alimony because I wanted it to be final so both of us could move on with our lives. However, that nest egg won't keep forever."

I continued cheerfully, "And now I get to take the time to write my book and get good coffee!" I say to get us back to present, as I don't want to start filling in a lot of detail that I'd have to remember later.

"I think we are going to have a great partnership here," he says confidently. "I'm sorry I was abrupt at first, some of that business callousness still resides. But hey, now that I'm thinking about it, I should have you meet Emma. Maybe the two of you could work out a deal for helping her teach English to the kids—that's her weak spot. I'd pay you, of course," he said quickly.

"I would love to meet your family. You just add more bags of coffee beans and computer time, and we'll call it even."

"Seems I'm not the only shrewd one here," he laughed. "Done."

I wondered if it was a mistake to meet his family. I knew I'll come to love them, adore Emma, and it would be a psychological shackle that would keep me here. Once I got on that computer, I needed to make sure to investigate Damon thoroughly. It wouldn't surprise me if Todd had him on the payroll as another means to hold me down.

After a couple more hours of reviewing clients, how to work the labels, and the general ledger, etc., I realized that I needed to get to my shift at the restaurant. We agreed on $150 per week in cash for working four mornings from eight to eleven and four hours on either Saturday or Sunday—my choice—and one night a week for tutoring after I met Emma. As I don't pay rent for my jail cell of a home, the money isn't important, but it is nest egg funds, untouchable in W-2 documents that Todd can't snoop into and find a way to take from me.

The credit cards Todd gave me initially were taken away, so now I pay for everything by cash. The nice Jeep Cherokee was replaced with my mountain bike and an old Chevy. "Can't let the good folks of Gardiner think you are anything but a lowly waitress." My money buys food, what I need for the house, gas for the car, and hope toward finding a way out of here.

Gardiner, Montana, population 3,200, is the perfect balance of being somewhat modern yet cloaked in privacy. It's so unlike most of the rural towns of my beloved Midwest, where everyone is into everyone else's business—at least that's what friends who were raised in the country tell me. Here, there seems to be a collective understanding that if you are choosing to live here, it is either to make money from the tourists or to live in happy, except in my case, solitude. I have lived all my life in various cities—Minneapolis, Chicago, Las Vegas, and now here. Sometimes my purpose gets lost in the Montana vastness. I do love this pristine frontier, though it too has been plagued with the Starbucks, Pizza Huts, and Wal-Marts. It is still so incredibly different than my helter-skelter life.

I had loved and hated my life. It was a precarious balance to say the least. The work I did led to some very dark worlds—places that, to this day, I cannot understand their existence or how people survive day in and day out and years on end, but they do. I shudder to think of how many buildings I have been in where people exist amongst rats and cockroaches; the sounds of fierce arguments; women and children crying; wires sparking out of dust-laden, overhead fluorescent lights; and the smells of stale urine and vomit nearly knocking one to the ground.

Dark places aren't always created by squalor. There is the darkness of opulence and overindulgence that nearly smothered me when I had assignments in Las Vegas. One doesn't get sucked into it when only there for a three-day convention or a long weekend. Those people are just getting a temporary escape from their normal, well-behaved lives. Danger to them is betting $100 on Texas Hold 'Em or finishing the drink in the four-foot vessel or flirting with the sales counterpart from the opposite part of the country. Knowing full well that "what happens in Vegas, stays in Vegas," they can giggle for two days, and then leave to go home to their families, barbecues, and PTA meetings.

However, over time the glitter of dangling diamonds cannot compensate for the dullness in the eyes of a prostitute or the desperation of the gambling addict, constantly looking over their shoulder for the goons employed by the unforgiving bookie. Everyone thinks the ridiculous amount of wealth flaunted on the blackjack tables, at Versace, and at the Ferrari dealership at Ceasar's equals happiness. The wealthy have their drudgery too. There is the unspoken requirement of needing to be seen with other "right" people, at the "right" places, sheathed by the "right" designers. This lifestyle leaves them just as bored and as soulless as the heroin addict in the slums of Chicago. This was the hate of my life—the sadness, the hopelessness, the shallowness, and the downright meanness. It all went against my Midwest sensibilities, or I suppose, my naivete.

It was Ron, my longtime editor, who educated me in the school of street smarts. I was a newspaper investigative reporter for twelve years, and I mostly loved it. Though my stories landed in several papers, they were all part of one media conglomerate, and Ron took care of me all those years. It was three years of minor stories—fires, car crashes, weird weather, page ten court cases, and so on. I worked my butt off, willing to take any story assigned to get noticed and, hopefully, move into the juicier stories—the ones that got on page two or page three.

It wasn't about wanting fame—very, very few newspaper writers achieve it, and those that do are ninety-nine percent columnists. But I didn't want to write fluff feature stories about the millionth new way to lose weight or on flower gardens, nor did I want to be a political columnist. It was always about the rush of find it first; first but accurate. All reporters in their baby stages will err, favoring speed over accuracy. Do enough of that and you are finished. You are allowed a couple faux pas, but that is it, because the next hungry, ambitious, starry-eyed reporter is on your heels, waiting to seize your spot.

I wish Ron were here now, or that I could communicate with him. I constantly try to figure my way out of here for good. Ron was the master of seeing every angle and every possible scenario or outcome. The mere fact that he hasn't found me tells me Todd is also a master at conjuring scenarios. Which means the promises of hurting John if I don't figure this out perfectly, are extremely possible.

Mara

One of the very few friends I have made here is Ellen Whitehair. Ellen is part of the Tribal Nation of the Crow, or their true name the Apsaaloke, which is the predominant tribal culture of South Central Montana.

Ellen is about ten years older than me, but she has the wisdom of the elders. She uses few words, but all are meaningful. Most Apsaaloke live on the reservation, and most still speak the native tongue as well as English. I find, like the other tribes I'm familiar with, such as the Chippewa, the Ojibwe, and the Lakota, the Apsaaloke have become more integrated with white culture, but cautiously.

Perhaps Ellen understands my pain and my need to be guarded. I don't denigrate either of us by thinking that if I wear some beaded necklaces, I get to be an honorary member of her tribe, any more than she becomes Gaelic for admiring Celtic crosses. I cannot stand people who think if they study a culture, it gives them the license to tattoo themselves in that culture's symbols because they "relate" to it. I am okay with everyone being Irish on St. Patrick's Day, though most use it as an excuse to get drunk, but I cringe when people get a Celtic knot tattoo because it is cool. Appreciate, admire, and respect a culture, just please, don't think you are part of it.

After my first few months here, and several conversations with Ellen at her booth at the Handcrafters & Farmers Market, she pulled out this amazing carved wooden pipe and a pottery bowl of sweet-smelling tobacco. She knows I smoke, something I did off and on in college and now all the time because of the stress and anxiety. She simply said, "Your tobacco is not blessed. It will not bring you peace. Take this." I tried to make a joke of it by replying, "Yeah, Marlboro isn't known for its healing powers."

Her face remained serious. Looking in her coal black eyes, I tried to discover why she would give me this very meaningful gift, but nothing gave a hint. Nowadays, I know she gets the same expressionless look if she is set on not talking, and I leave whatever I'm trying to glean from her alone. I thanked her for the gift and nodded, tears forming. Within my soul, I know she knows the depth of my troubles. What they are exactly is not important to her.

I waited a few weeks to reciprocate. To do so immediately would only look like payback and would diminish her offering as a true gift. Those of us who are Celtic by ancestry use clan instead of tribe, but there are similarities. Though it probably wasn't the brightest thing to do, I brought the only Celtic remnants I had with me to her booth. The first is a Claddaugh ring. It has an inscription of "Beigh la eile ag an bPaorach," which means "We will live another day." The other is a blanket that goes with me anytime I travel. It has my family's crest woven on it along with the saying "Is I ding di fein a scoileann an dair." It translates to "It is a wedge of itself that splits the oak." I interpret it to mean "Beware of the enemy within." It is the ring that I will give her along with the interpretation and leave it at that.

What I like so much about Ellen is there is no insecurity in the relationship. If I don't see or speak to her for a few weeks at a time, it's no big deal. We don't sip coffee at each other's homes. I have no wish to supplement my curiosity by asking to visit the inner dwellings of the reservation, and she respects my privacy as well.

Our relationship may not have a history, nor does it have the benefit of knowing the ins and outs of the other person. But, Ellen knows all is not what it seems, and yet her body language, her actions, and the few words she does use, tell me that she knows it is not my fault. I have not spelled out my situation to anyone. I'm not a natural-born liar, but my reporting experience has given me a poker face, the ability to control my body language so as not to give anything away, and of course, practice keeping a secret.

Mara

In mid-March, Gardiner sees the last of the die-hard skiers, and then there is a lull until late April, when the hikers begin arriving. The air is a little bit warmer, the ferocious bite of winter slowly disappearing. Ellen told me the howls of the winter winds are the ancient cries for loves lost, taken by starvation, avalanches, or just the cold itself.

The restaurant is at expected levels of busyness. Customers are decent and tip well. I had worked both lunch and dinner the day before and had a raging headache. After gulping down two Advil, I open the front door to retrieve mail from the nondescript black metal mailbox. I throw the small stack on my little wrought iron kitchen table.

I don't have any bills. Good old Todd, generous guy that he is, has paid for everything in my luxurious surroundings. Any mail I get is 98 percent junk. There's a flyer for the local grocery store—I leaf through it, looking for coupons, and out drops a letter.

There is no return address, and the stamp says it was sent from California. I get a letter with a photo of John every few weeks from Todd, and every time the stamp is from a different state, indicating no solid evidence of where Todd is presently. I shake as I open the envelope. I'm terrified this time the photo will reveal John ashen with his eyes permanently closed. When I see he is alive, I start to sob out of a combination of relief, anxiety, and renewed fear.

The picture was taken at least 40 to 50 feet away, but it's clearly him. I stroke the flat image of his dark hair and touch his face. I want to believe that by some great lovers' connectivity, he can feel me from here. I want him to feel the hot tears splashing on him. I quickly wipe the photo, so as not to ruin it.

I don't want to read the note. I cannot stand to see or touch anything Todd has touched. I hate him with the blackest, darkest part of me. For cold comfort, I daydream of his demise. I wish for a car accident that injures him in such a way that he suffers and slowly bleeds to death. I dream of him entrapped in a fire, choking and suffocating toxic fumes, meanwhile every inch of him is encased in burning flesh, hoping he is howling and crying in pain, then maybe, just maybe, he feels what I feel, what I feel every single day.

My anger is the only way I can get through this. I'm not afraid of him anymore per se, though I now know what he is capable of. I know he will carry out his threat if I screw up. I have to read the note to make sure this one doesn't have some sort of direction I have to follow. Every note contains his verbal abuse, his mockery, and his efforts to humiliate me. This note is no different, always typed.

My Dearest Mara—

I am pleased that you continue to do as you are told. As you can see, John is still alive. I must admit I am impressed by the fortitude you both are showing. But not for long. This picture was taken outside a local restaurant. John was meeting your friends and, it looks like, a single woman. I saw her as they left. He was smiling. She is quite gorgeous. I'll send another picture of them together.

I think you will agree they make a handsome couple. Maybe he is realizing you aren't coming back; that you are dead to him. Maybe he thinks it is time to bury Mara and start a new life. Maybe he dreams of her at night now, and not you. Maybe he dreams of marrying her. Think of that, Mara! John having a new wife! Wouldn't you love that for him?

And what would happen to you? If he does remarry, then maybe I would consider letting you leave. After all, John doesn't seem the type to divorce, even if it was for you. He'd realize he fell in love with someone else and that you are of his past.

His sorrow has run deep for you. You wouldn't be so selfish as to come back into his life after he had the courage to try love again, correct?

Hope you are making good tips at the restaurant! I might even have to order a pound of coffee from the roaster you are working for. It's good that you are working hard and honorably now.

—Todd

I run to the bedroom and scream into my pillow until it hurts. I pull out the baseball bat I keep for protection and repeatedly hit the mattress until my arms and shoulders are numb. At the end of my tirade, I slump to the floor and cry until there is no liquid left. When I open my eyes again, I see that the sky is turning from periwinkle to dark blue. My muscles hurt; my head feels there is a rock hitting it over and over. My throat is parched.

Forcing myself to the kitchen, I grab another three Advil and gulp down two glasses of water. I want to be drunk, high, anything to be relieved of this pain, if only for a short time. Sometimes I give in to the clear, fluid escape that vodka provides. Most of the time, I walk away from the temptation because I need to remain sharp. I must be ready for his misstep, my exit from this exile. I'm angry I haven't figured out how to escape this nightmare.

Tonight hurt. I know the taunting won't end, and I've tried to harden myself, to not let it get to me. Usually, I can just tear up the letter, scream, cry, and then move on, choosing to focus on John's handsome face; handsome while becoming a little more gaunt, hollow.

Todd is a master manipulator. He knew tonight would hurt. I'm sure he was exuberant in this. Maybe I'll drink tonight, even though I'll pay for it tomorrow. Who cares? That's tomorrow. For now, oblivion may be the only thing that will keep me from getting in the car and driving, without stopping, until I see John in the flesh again. You win again, asshole.

WHOOSH.

Eyes wide open, I look around wildly, coughing and choking, breathing hard through my nose, trying to calm down. The clock says 2:15 a.m. Another dream, generated from the latest letter and photo. It isn't a nightmare—nightmares aren't real. The various scenes from the past months keep playing over and over, in no particular sequence. I head to the kitchen for a glass of water, as I obviously have forgotten how dehydrated vodka makes me. Taking the water with me, I head to the living room, curl up on the couch, and stare out the window into the black abyss.

It is unreal how long this has played out. My nerves are raw. I still cannot understand Todd's obsession. How much hatred does this guy have? I cannot understand this kind of crazy. How does he live like this? Not that I care if he lives at all, but how does he do normal things, like go to his office every day? Does he make small talk with the cashier at the grocery store, knowing he has a hostage? How does he have the steely nerves for it?

Why the hell am I giving him any thought? Because you just relived a piece of it again, Mara. Even after all this time, I will not refer to myself as Anne. I keep hoping, believing this will end. I could be Mara again, for real, for good. Yet something in my gut tells me that it will only end when I figure out how to connect to John without endangering him. There won't be any parole from the lunatic. The thought that it could last years brings forth the tears. No racking sobs, just a steady flow of water trickling down my face, down to the threadbare, khaki-colored couch, leaving dark, wet drops.

Subconsciously chewing on my thumbnail, I think about the pattern of this game. I work, temporarily forgetting about my situation, while my head fills with requests for crispy bacon, dressing on the side, and dry martinis. My life drones on this way for a few weeks, then I get the letter, go into a panic and fall apart, and then it starts all over again.

I have tried to think of ways out. I try to think of ways I could get a message to John without Todd finding out. Maybe I've given him too much credit, as I shoot down idea after idea. He has proven to be wickedly meticulous and street smart, not at all the young man I went to homecoming with in high school.

It is all I can do from becoming utterly hopeless, from giving up completely. My core says that all that crap about John and a new woman is just another weapon in this psychological war. But then doubt creeps in. What if John has moved on? What if he has started dating again? I can't be so arrogant to think he's created a shrine to my memory and avowed celibacy.

I smile, thinking of how he proposed. He dressed up like a Gaelic warrior for a Halloween party, kilt and all, and in the traditional commando fashion. During the height of the party, he demanded silence as he shouted in the worst Irish accent ever, "Hear ye, hear ye. Amongst us, is a princess, no, a queen. Mara, house of Riley."

I was blushing furiously and whispered, "John, shut up already." But of course, he didn't.

"Mara, house of Riley," he said as he got on one knee, not realizing or caring that the quick move to the knee caused his kilt to fly up, briefly exposing his, um, gifts. "I am but a humble man—a man who loves you," he said, losing his Irish accent, "and for the rest of our days, I'm asking in front of all our friends, if you'll join the House of Finegan." And with that, he pulled a box from the pouch that hung from his swash buckle, which he opened and presented a titanium band carved with a Gaelic weave with a gorgeous emerald and diamond setting in the middle.

I was stunned. It was one of the few times in my life that I was speechless. I didn't see the crowd around us or hear the music, the only thing I was aware of was the warmth in his eyes. I didn't need to think. I smiled so wide my face hurt, and I leapt to his bended knee and kissed him my answer. The one thing no one can take is our memories.

John

I am going, though in protest. I hate being the fifth wheel. I'm sick of the pity. As if they believe I can't feel the glances between them. As if I don't know that they think I'm nuts.

But they are my friends, our friends. Veronica DuMonde is one of Mara's best friends. Her husband, Emile, and I hit it off right away at their wedding, my tenth date with Mara. Emile and I shared several jokes along with several cocktails. Then there is Ed and Lorraine Mansfield. Ed is practically my brother and now my business partner. An all-around super guy, who married a super gal. And of course, Jay and Mallory and Sean and Monica.

Our life was perfect.

Part of me thinks Veronica is being completely disloyal to Mara. She and the others are dragging me to this new restaurant where I am going to meet this chick Veronica works with. The chick is my age and a widow—in my presumably same predicament. The problem is, I'm not a widower.

I don't think I can do this. I don't think I can give up on her yet.

I feel so guilty, allowing myself to laugh with everyone and Tara? Tricia? I could see the dullness in her eyes too, a reflection of my own. Thank God Veronica and Emile can talk about anything and without pause without being ill at ease or awkward.

"So, Tricia, tell John about your family's business," Emile says with flourish. Emile, though born in the United States, is so, so very much his French heritage. He has an upbeat lilt in his voice, and performing any task in relation to wine is like being able to drive a clutch while smoking a cigarette and drinking coffee. He pours Tricia a glass of Merlot, the fourth bottle he ordered for the group, as a prompt to get her to talk.

She flusters a little bit then says, "Emile makes it sound as if the family business is like being in the Mafia or even more extravagant than it is." She takes a sip of wine, then dabs her heart-shaped lips with her napkin.

"My family is from Virginia. Our line of McNeils settled in Chesapeake Bay in the early 1700s."

"Scottish, then?" I ask.

She smiles. "Very much so, but over time, I think it has watered down a bit." Her smile widens. "I don't think we'll have any clan issues over dinner, right?"

At first, I am struck with how she somehow tapped into my brain. Mara and I are avowed Irish with an ancient distaste for the Scottish, who helped sell out Ireland to the British. I feel my cheeks redden, then in the whole three seconds that actually passed, I soften at her teasing remark and reply, "No clan politics here. I mean, if we can have the French as friends," as I nod to Emile, "then you and I can surely get along."

"Here, here," chimes Veronica, raising her glass. "Here's to all of us and friendships."

We toast and smile at one another. With Veronica and Emile, you are guaranteed lighthearted conversation, woven with sincerity and laughter. I'm certain those two even disagree with each other with a smile on their faces.

Emile, our unofficial host, brought us back to Tricia, wanting to hear more of her family's immigration tale. "Please, Tricia, forgive us. We have group ADD. Let's hear the story."

She finished a bite of her ciabatta roll and proceeded, "Our family were blacksmiths and artisans. Much of the beautiful wrought iron you see incorporated in the Southern plantation architecture and the Presbyterian churches, can probably be traced to a McNeil."

Veronica pipes in, "I just find all of that, despite its purposes, so beautiful. I am always amazed how they shaped the iron in such perfect twists and points."

Tricia addresses this, "It is a matter of hitting the iron with the right tool at the right time and at the right temperature. The cooling of it has to be accurate too."

I spoke up, "Even more so, I'm curious about how they mined iron, how they came to know its properties, how they figured out how to work it."

"John, I hate to disappoint, but that is where I no longer can claim any working knowledge. Too technical for me," she said.

I took an opportunity to tease back, "So too much of a guy thing for you?"

"Touché." We all laughed.

The evening went smoothly. I treated myself to a filet with a mushroom sauce. It was delectable. I'm not a bad cook, but I don't make much off the range of soups, sandwiches, and salads. Occasionally, I make pasta or a steak, but all the love and preparation seem to be a waste for one. Tricia had either salmon or swordfish, I forget which. She eats delicately. She is a lovely woman—honey amber hair, brown eyes, and gorgeous lips. Lips that would be heavenly to enjoin with mine.

Cripes, John. I shake my head, as if shaking away a swarm of gnats. *You fucking pig. How can you think that? Because it has been nearly a year since you've had sex,* says a voice in my head. Pissed at myself for having carnal thoughts about Tricia while still married to Mara, I open a bottle of Harp's and flop on the couch. I call it a weakness, maybe even a test. Till death do us part. I catch myself twisting the wedding band that is emotionally fused to my finger; the real one is on my dresser. I sit forward and take two swigs of the beer.

It is wrong for me to flirt. It is wrong for me to be attracted to Tricia. She seemed nice, funny, pretty, and bright. In all honesty, the Scottish thing doesn't bother me. It could be—she could be a vegan.

FUCK! Stop it already! The bottom of the beer bottle hits the table a bit too hard and a chip falls to the floor. But I don't care. Twenty minutes later, I look up from having my head down in my hands. Initially, my sight is blurry, with little colored dots flying in front of my eyes. I stand up a bit abruptly, feeling lightheaded, and wander to the kitchen for another beer.

Mara

I'm not good at faking it. For the short term, maybe, anyone can. Long term is too exhausting; it requires too much effort. In this small community, though, it is normal. You get what you see, and no one seems to care; everyone is embedded in their own world with their own problems.

For the time I am in the public eye, I can pull it off. I can be friendly and sincere. I can make small talk and joke around with customers. In a way, work is an escape, even if it is a facade. I never fully let my guard down, but the weight of my problems is awarded a reprieve during these blocks of time. But once I clock out, it is as if I unzip out of that skin and the real me is revealed. The me that has deep lines forming on my forehead, the me with more gray in my hair. The me with heavy eyes, lacking any spark.

Even though I'm tired, I'm glad I rode my mountain bike to work. It isn't that far, but the few minutes in the late spring night air fill my lungs with icy air, causing me to breathe harder, which, surprisingly, refreshes my brain.

I don't understand the human condition as much as I thought I did. I don't know when or how or even if this cycle will ever end, and yet, I continue trying to survive it. What if there is no end? What if this is it? What if there is no John when it's over? Then I have nothing to live for. I just exist because psychically, and physically, the body will do whatever it takes to survive. It will stave off death until the last possible thread is cut. Suicide takes an enormous amount of willpower and a complete utter depletion of hope.

I pedal harder. My backpack contains only my uniform, my purse, and a bottle of water. I wish I could push out the thoughts and pedal my way through the madness of it all. The adrenaline feels good; good being a relative thing. Adrenaline makes me more powerful, more willing to fight. Though it is a little more challenging to navigate the roads in the dark, I don't care. I make the decision to ride through the North Entrance of Yellowstone, flashing my badge to the ranger on duty in the booth, and head toward Mammoth Hot Springs. It's a quick jaunt of a few miles; I'll just turn around after I hit it.

The darkness is utterly black and consumptive. It gives me confidence, which combines with the adrenaline to make me fearless. It fills my bravery jar with coin. Stretching my resolve that this will end. That I will figure out an answer. That one day, I will be back in

John's arms.

————

Forty-five minutes later, I'm back in the house. My ears ache from the chilled air and my throat is a little raw, but I don't care. My brain finally decided to wake up from this semi-coma I allowed. I couldn't think of solutions because I was too busy being angry or sad or feeling sorry for myself.

I was a cross-country runner until my knees gave out in high school. I wasn't a competitive contender by any means, but it gave me focus, mental stamina, and determination. The mind can adapt to whatever it is given and told to do. I would tell myself that if I can run five miles, I can run ten. I would focus on the next horizon in front of me and the next and the next. I solved a lot of problems this way. While I cannot run anymore, the bike is now the vehicle I can use to build up my mind again. Hope is a powerful weapon. I'm going to use all my tools, and I'm going to end this. I'm going to find a way to get some sort of message to John. The very idea of it has me smiling, smiling for real.

I needed to be calm. I needed to not rush to conclusions or rush through a process. I need to play like a champion chess genius— thinking out all my moves, Todd's countermoves, be at least eight to ten steps ahead of the game. I have all the time in the world, I tell myself, over and over as a mantra.

Although I did this once when my sentence began, I spend the next two hours tearing the house apart, combing every inch for a bug or a camera. I go through every drawer and cabinet, take off every vent cover and lamp shade, gloss my fingers through the curtains, take apart the back of the old television and the cover of the dishwasher, and unscrew every light bulb, looking in each of the sockets. I get on my hands and knees to feel for any weird bumps in the floors and then take my hands over every wall for any cracks.

Exhausted, yet vitalized from the conclusion that Todd left the inside of the house alone, I started making lists. Lists are how I take things from my head and make sense of them. I listed everyone John and I knew. I tried to list every client John had from the memory of our conversations —I understood this list wouldn't be complete, but it was a start. I tried to remember every story I wrote over the last couple of years. As I went through these exercises, I was oblivious to time. I finally looked at my watch and saw that it was 4 a.m.

My stomach was rumbling, and I could feel myself getting lightheaded. The only way I was going to succeed was to take care of myself physically. If I did that, my brain would work better too. During the hours that all this manifested, I had changed. I wasn't going to be the hapless, hopeless victim. I was going to beat this bastard one way or another. More than anything, I had to shut off my feelings, good or bad, and become steely cold. I had to detach.

While I had some bread toasting, I decide I need to clean out anything getting in my way. I threw out the bottles of vodka and tequila. I even threw out the pouches of strong herbs from Ellen. It wasn't marijuana, but it most certainly had the same soothing, mind butter affect. I had almost thrown out the Mountain Dew, then I stopped and laughed at myself. Being awake and alert fell on the good side of the attributes I now needed to have and to hone. No more junk food. Though I wasn't overweight or even pudgy, I knew that all the fat and sugar would make me sluggish.

I finally called it quits and exhaled as I fell back onto the couch. The spike in adrenaline wore me out. My spirit wanted to keep going, but my body threw up the white flag. I saw no harm in taking a break, as I had the day off from both the restaurant and the Roastery. I switched on the television and even after only a few minutes, my eyelids grew heavy and I surrendered to the sweet escape of sleep.

Mara

The computer is spitting out labels for the Old Faithful run of beans. Chipper as always, Damon greets me with a smile. "Hey, Anne. What brings you here today? I didn't think you were coming until tomorrow."

"I was going to look into some potential hikes outside of Yellowstone," I lie. "While I'm here, I'll just do the orders that I had planned for tomorrow."

He nods. "Cool. In fact, that would be awesome. Did I tell you that we have a new client?"

While my intent is to do some other research that I'm impatient to start, I need to play along. I put a smile on my face and say, "No, tell me about it!"

"So, a few months ago I started making some calls to Glacier Park. Emma has a cousin who married a ranger, and I chatted with him a couple times to see who he knew there. Come to find out his uncle owns property outside the West Gate. He has fifteen cabins for vacationers. Yadda, yadda, yadda, after some introductions and making a couple of trips, not only do I get an in with this guy but also with the owners of the big resort in Apgar Village.

"Two weeks ago, I did a presentation of two blends that would be just for Glacier. We agreed that Apgar Village and Uncle Walt would get exclusive selling privileges for this season and then the following season we could market to the whole damn area. Yesterday we got the final yes." His happiness radiates through every pore of his body.

"Oh my God, that is great!" I genuinely exclaim. "When does it all go into motion?"

"The new roaster arrives tomorrow. It'll take a couple of weeks to get it adjusted for mass production. It was a risk ordering it ahead of the sale, but I felt good about it. I've been spending extra time doing small batches to get the blend consistent. But the packaging design is ready. Emma went with me two trips ago and took some breathtaking photos and made lots of sketches. We got approval on the names and packaging last week."

I am truly impressed. "How did you keep this under wraps for so long?" I tease him. "You know you don't have the best poker face—or maybe you do, since I had no clue."

"Anne, you've been on a different planet these last weeks. You seemed preoccupied, so I figured something was on your mind and when you were ready, you'd be on board. That, and I didn't want to jinx myself." He winks at me.

"Congratulations! I'm really happy for you! So, when do I get to ask for a raise?" I joke.

He stiffens a little. "I would love to do that, but I want to pay off the roaster first."

"I was just kidding, Damon," I say as I give him a gentle punch to the bicep. "You know I'm not leaving you." Not anytime soon, I think silently.

He brightens up again. "Okay, whew! Thanks for understanding. Gotta get back to the grind." He laughs at his pun as I roll my eyes. "But hey, since you said you're here to do a little work, it would be totally awesome to get this stack of orders ready to go."

This stack contains twenty orders, which will take me two to three hours to do. While I'm anxious to get on the computer, this won't derail me from my research. I just need to get it done, and then look out, enemy mine, my search will begin. My profile is Cork23Bridge. Cork for the county in Ireland my family is from; 23 represents 1923, the year my family came to America; and Bridge for Bridgit nee Donovan, my maternal grandmother. I hope it is random enough to not send out any warning signals to Todd.

Finally, I was able to start my search. I had time, which meant I needed to keep my anxiety in check so I could be extraordinarily thorough. I began my search with every known tech firm in Wichita, Kansas. I had learned during another tedious search that Todd had his first job in Wichita. Every IT, hardware, software, and consulting firm was now under my scrutiny. I spent hours diving deep into Facebook and LinkedIn accounts— looking through friends of friends of friends. At twenty-one, even Todd didn't have the level of maturity or sophistication to wipe away all his footprints.

I went to the website of every company I could find in the digital white pages and Dun and Bradstreet. First, I searched their "About Us" section to see if Todd's name surfaced. Most companies only list the executive officers, and knowing his social and leadership limitations I didn't think his name would be among them, but I had to try anyway.

For three hours, I poured over the websites of more than sixty-two companies on my list. Nothing. Wichita may not be a hopping metropolis, but the parameters of my search yielded more than 200 more companies to review. My eyes were glazed and hunger was gnawing at me, so I reluctantly concluded today's research, a little disappointed.

I also didn't want to take advantage of Damon and his generosity, nor possibly involve him in my search. I could not allow any possibility of harm to Damon or his family if Todd somehow found out about his involvement, however innocent. After erasing my searches and properly ejecting the flash drive that contained the list of remaining companies to review, I shut down the computer and purposefully walked into Damon's office to tell him goodbye and thank him for the computer time.

"No problem, Anne. It's not like I get charged for usage. I'm amazed you can sit in front of a computer for that long. Can't stand being on it myself." He smiled. "I hope you found what you were looking for."

I lied and said, "I did." I said a bit too enthusiastically. "So thanks again."

He stood up and said, "When I'm zeroed in like that, I abandon bodily needs like food and sleep. I was going to grab a burger at Porky's—want to join me?"

I wanted to say no, but hunger was beginning to get the best of me, and I didn't want to be rude, so I replied, "That's nice of you, sure, but I rode my bike. I can meet you there if you give me a head start."

"Nah, let's just strap the bike to the rack."

I gave in, and after a few minutes spent getting the bike situated, we took off. It was nice to escape my reality in small talk and a bacon cheeseburger. Inwardly, I was happy and a touch envious about his life with Emma. Hearing his stories, basic domestic stories one takes for granted, made me ache for John. I didn't think the tale of a broken toilet chain could tug at my heart as it did. After forty-five minutes or so, we both claimed exhaustion and got ready to leave. Ever the gentleman, Damon insisted on driving me home, as it was now dark outside.

"Can't have you knock over a moose or a tourist on that thing," he joked as he unsecured my bike from his car and carried it onto my small screened porch.

"Thanks again, Damon, for everything. I really appreciate it." I genuinely meant.

"Least I can do for someone willing to work on a day off and listen to my plumbing woes," he offered.

I waved as the headlights pulled out of the driveway and he headed to his sanctuary of domestic bliss, leaving me to another lonely night.

Part 4

One Year Later - John

For some strange reason, I have this sick feeling again. I didn't eat anything weird last night, surprisingly, and haven't drank anything, and yet I feel awful. And now I need to puke.

I barely made it to the bathroom, stomach tight as if I did 500 crunches and dripping in sweat. Must be the flu. Great. I absolutely cannot cancel any of the meetings scheduled for tomorrow.

Scrolling through Facebook as I sip some water, I get one of those "On This Day" notifications. My heart about comes up through my throat. It is a picture of Mara and I having dinner with our crew from three years ago. We look so happy. I look healthier than I do now. I didn't even notice until one of my team asked if I should go see a doctor. Apparently, I've lost weight and have deeper lines around my eyes.

Then the reason for my sudden vomiting hits me. Tomorrow is the one-year mark of the day she left. No, leaving implies that she intended not to return, that she intended to disappear. She didn't. I still cannot accept that she's dead. But then I struggle—if she isn't dead, then why hasn't she returned? And the whole series of thoughts come back to torture me.

Maybe she's living a double life. Maybe she doesn't want to be found. Maybe she never loved me and found someone else. She's extremely resourceful. She could have faked her death. But the suitcase and the Jeep had her blood on them. Given the photos of where the Jeep was found, amongst the craggy rocks, no one could have survived that, —only an expert could have climbed out from there, which she was not.

I keep thinking she has been wandering around with amnesia. What if she somehow did survive and is now living a different life, with no recollection of her life here? Wouldn't something deep in her subconscious tell her that something wasn't right? That everything was foreign?

I can't help myself. I pull out the thick folder of all the work done by the detective and start going through it for the hundredth time. I feel guilty for not having looked through it in a couple of months. But maybe with the time that has elapsed, I can find or see something, anything that doesn't make sense.

There are the photos of the parking lot where she left her car to get the car she was to use for her travel. These came from the store's video surveillance. We were lucky to get those at all, as most places dump their surveillance footage after a couple of weeks. I see her getting out of her car and loading her stuff into the Jeep; I see her take off. Nothing indicating which way she was heading.

I look at the photos of her car. The car was returned to the house while I was gone, and I have no idea who returned it or how the driver got back to wherever. The only prints collected were hers and mine. The driver must have worn gloves. There were no hair strands, no unusual fibers, no bodily fluids either, nothing that would have belonged to the third person.

I look at the photos of the suitcase. It most definitely was hers, as it was brightly colored and her initials were etched in the top near the handle. The identity card was missing, but I imagine she removed it as a precaution against someone figuring out who she really was. I ponder all this hard, so hard that I don't realize my fists are clenched and I'm shaking. Holy shit. What if?

What if she was never meant to be found? What if . . . ? I start pacing around as the overflow of thoughts take over, scrambling in my head. I pull up the pictures of the suitcase again. I see the etched initials again. What am I missing? I stare and stare. I get that feeling like when the right word just can't make it to the tongue. I know there is something missing, but I can't see it. I stare again. Nothing. Crap!

I slam the pictures down. I go to grab a beer, and I'm pulled toward our junk drawer in the kitchen. I forget the beer and yank everything out. A box of buttons, a spool of white thread, a jar opener, rubber bands, tape, straws, AAA batteries, two potholders woven by my niece, unused balloons from some party we threw, a compact mirror, and a magnet with our dentist's logo on it are now sprawled on the counter.

The magnet has a cheesy drawing of a person with a large toothy smile. A smile. What about a smile? A picture in her car with a smile? Something about a toothbrush? Dental floss? An appointment?

Oh God.

I run back to the pictures of the suitcase. I look at all of them again. I don't see it. I don't see it anywhere. And suddenly, a tiny, fragmented spark of hope hits me. The stupid, dorky, orange smiley face sticker is missing. It should be on the right-hand corner of the front pocket. It's not there.

IT'S NOT THERE!!!!!!

Dear God, is this a clue? Could it possibly NOT be her suitcase? I hold my breath and clasp both hands over my mouth. How did I miss this? How did we all miss this? I look again at the etched initials. It's too small to confidently tell if it's the same. But the damn sticker is gone. It could have fallen off. No, no it couldn't have because my beloved OCD wife taped over it so it couldn't fall off.

What else isn't right? The possibilities are making my heart race. The nausea has been replaced with butterflies. I run to my briefcase and pull out the pad of sketch paper I keep for doing preliminary designs with clients. My hand is shaking as I'm trying to find a pencil. Where are my glasses? Shit. I can't find a damn thing.

Just calm down, John, you have the whole day. Shit, I'm supposed to go to my brother's this afternoon. I'll call him and say I'm down with the flu—I did puke, right? Not lying. Can't tell anyone anything yet until I have more than the suddenly very beautiful orange sticker as evidence.

Mara

After hours of pouring over companies and figuring out Todd's path since college, I realize the effort was pointless and wasn't going to get me what I wanted: his vulnerability. No matter how meticulous someone is, no one is perfect at not leaving any missteps. As much as it repulsed me, I had to start thinking like him. I needed to get into his head.

As frustrating as this task was, I was deeply motivated. I had nothing to lose and everything to gain. But I had to keep it to myself. I couldn't let it show when I was at work. I couldn't let my hope show in my expressions outside of the shack I was living in, lest I was being watched. I needed to put on the facade of being broken. After this much time, I was willing to bet that if I appeared as he wanted me to be, then his guard would go down.

The letters and pictures came less frequently. As much as his barbs and taunts still hurt, I lived for the pictures, even though they showed John gaunt and tired and expressionless at times. Narcissistic as it seems, if John still looked down, then it meant he wasn't ready to move on yet. I still had time.

As much as I wanted to find ways to hurt Todd, my efforts were starting to focus more on how to reach out to John without raising suspicion. Hurting Todd was a daydream I allowed myself periodically. I thought about ways of somehow sending an anonymous letter to the FBI, telling them they should investigate him, as I'd gamble that he earned his money illegally, but Todd would know it was me, and who knows what alias he used in his work life.

I thought of hiring an assassin with the cash I had saved and hidden. But that was laughable since I only had $2,500 saved. Plus, death would be too easy, and after being imprisoned here, I wasn't about to get thrown in jail, nor did I really have a killer instinct. I knew my hatred could distract me and cause me to make mistakes, ones I could not afford. It made me think of the R.E.M song "Living Well Is the Best Revenge." I decided I needed to be able to live with myself when this was over. One thing was absolutely certain: this nightmare would end, and it would end with me looking right into the bastard's eyes.

My job then, was to continue waiting tables, continue working at the Roastery, continue tutoring Damon's children, just continue. In doing so, I felt lighter than I had in months, both physically and emotionally. Riding the bike as much as possible toned me up, giving me a more sinuous look than I'd had in a long time. Emotionally? Hope is an amazing drug. It gives me purpose. It gives me a sense of excitement and joy. It made it possible to get out of bed in the morning. At the same time, it forced me to be disciplined with my emotions, as patience was the weapon I needed the most.

Emma, Damon's wife, is one of the most amazing moms I've ever met. She has a confidence that made me comfortable that she was comfortable with the working relationship I had with her husband. Damon and Emma were too melded with each other—no outsider would ever be able to break that. I understood completely. As lonely as my life had become without John, I had no interest in any other man, including Damon. I was still careful about what information I provided to him, though I believe that if he knew the story, he would help me. But then again, I had been fooled by Matthew, the "real estate agent" who worked for Todd. I hope one day I will be able to fully trust people again.

Damon, however, trusted me. I got my own set of keys and could work anytime of the day, instead of set hours. He even permitted nighttime work, which was perfect for doing investigative work while labels for coffee bags churned out, and it helped on the nights filled with insomnia. I drove the car at nights, as I really didn't want to meet up with an elk in heat on my bike. After Damon won the Glacier National Park bid, we were busy all the time. The additional roaster allowed Damon to seek out new business once a month, and we gained two more additional clients. *We.* I need to be careful about that word.

Shortly after gaining the additional two clients, Damon asked me to give up the restaurant job and be there full time. "I either get you full time or I need to hire another part-time employee, and I'm just not ready to expand the family business."

I was momentarily taken aback. He now considered me part of his family. My heart was torn. On the one side, to have connectivity to a group of people that unconditionally love you is so reassuring. But when you are grieving and aching for the family that you share DNA, a lifetime of memories, and an imprint of them in your mind and heart that cultivates the core of who you are, well, then, it is terribly bittersweet.

But outwardly, without pause, I gave Damon a joyous and thankful yes. In doing so, I felt the heartstring ties unravel just the tiniest bit.

My mother and father have been my rocks all my life. My mother blessed me with her wisdom, did not hover, and was unafraid to comfort when needed. My dad gave me humor and an optimistic but realistic view of the world. Neither of them tried to talk me out of being a journalist, though they expressed their concerns and pointed out the potential viciousness that life could lead.

"You will always have to find ways to balance yourself," my dad said. "Whether it's going to a feel good movie, sitting amongst a field of flowers, or doing charitable work."

I didn't really understand that. "I'm going to be a crusader for justice, for unheard voices—where is the darkness in that?" I asked.

"Because, Mara, in order to find justice, you have to wallow in the unjust, the ugly, and the horrible to know what justice would look like. I just don't want to see you turn hard and callous—I want my baby girl to keep her sunny disposition about life. That overall, life is beautiful."

"But that's the point, Dad, everyone should get a chance to have a beautiful life. And some start out so pitifully, I just want to find ways, through exposing the corrupt, to give those people a chance."

"But what you'll also have to remember is that some people have chosen to turn their back on hope. Hope requires risk, and there are some that would rather be miserable than take a risk. There will be people who you will not be able to help. Some people really have to take their own first steps before your help will have any impact."

I've thought about that conversation more than once during my imprisonment. Not always about helping myself out of this situation, but about why Todd would take such risks. I wonder if he has been disappointed that the climax he may have been imagining, didn't happen. I didn't beg. I overcame being broken. All the time he spent planning this, what a waste. I found myself pitying him. A life of hate and revenge could only destroy a person—what reward has all of this brought him? He couldn't be in such denial that he believed the level of intense psychological warfare could last indefinitely, could he?

Which then made me wonder. Would he truly cause John harm? Would he really kill him? Was he so far gone from the God of his childhood that his depraved belief of following it through was today's God's plan? I wasn't completely sure I was ready to chance that just yet. I had to come up with a micro test. One so small that it could be done under the radar but also potentially be missed by John. I had to wonder if I had the creativity and the nerve to try.

What was so special about me that my high school break-up sent Todd this far over the edge? Surely at eighteen there wasn't a halo over my head or an aura of light that made me somehow "holy" in his eyes. Did I promise him too much? Was I too cruel in our parting? I simply didn't answer his phone calls or read the letters he sent. I imagine that after I left for college my parents just chucked any letters he sent to my house and didn't tell me, which was fine. Except, maybe it would have produced clues as to how we got here.

Or maybe he was born with a confused mind, his warped sense of being cultivated by his parents' religious fanaticism. How many have committed treachery in the name of religion? In that sense, I could see how people have turned their backs on God, as if He were the author of such beguilement. I can't help but believe that God made things simple, articulated through Christ—love one another as you love yourself. But if one is filled with self-loathing, fear, and anger, then wouldn't all the man-made laws, declared as from God, come forth to fill a hole for those feelings, to falsely provide a sense of self-righteousness and superiority over others? It has to be something like this because, again, the God I believe in gave me free will, which means this imprisonment cannot possibly be ordained.

Several months ago, when I was still in disbelief and feared I'd be here forever, I had thought about all of my shortcomings, of the things I have done wrong. I had started down the path of thinking maybe I did deserve this. When in fear, the mind can be twisted and go to some dark places. Like anyone, I've made some bad choices, I've lost my temper, I've said mean things, I can be selfish, but I don't think my heart has ever had bad intentions. I don't think my desire to seek justice equaled wanting harm. I don't wish all the murderers and pedophiles to be tortured to death, just locked up for good.

It took a while, but when I went through all this soul searching, I concluded that it wasn't me. Obviously, I'm not perfect, nor ever will be, but I was not responsible for the situation I was in. Todd has a soul sickness that has taken over. There is no rationale to be found in such a person's actions. My job then, was not to think of the logical thing he would do but instead to prepare for the illogical and emotional. I keep making the mistake that cold-blooded killers are without emotion, otherwise how could they do what they do—it is the opposite, they are overly emotional.

I'm pondering this more as I weed out the little garden I had created. I had started it to create some beauty within my prison. It was months before I realized that I despised the house because of what it represented, not the actual house itself. I bought a few framed paintings and photos of the landscape. I purchased a couple of sky blue and lime green pillows for the pathetic couch.

I made a small garden in the front yard in the spring. Damon had given me his old lawnmower, and I found a good shovel at the hardware store. Emma, the kids, and I spent a couple of hours at the farmers market, carefully selecting a colorful variety of wildflower annuals: yellow Balsamroot, red Prairie Smoke, and blue Aster now brightened my lot.

As tempting as it is to pick bouquets from the vast fields of flowers, Yellowstone absolutely forbids it. The flowers at the farmers market all come from individuals who grow on their own property—they sell at the market, but Yellowstone purchases a good chunk too, to replace what was too tempting to poachers. As I am not a flora expert, I greatly appreciate the care and dedication the park has in keeping the landscape wild.

I had thought about trying to grow vegetables, as I missed my own raised garden at home. There I had rosemary, cilantro, lettuce, carrots, cherry and pear tomatoes, green beans, and jalapenos. Emma told me that while she applauded the idea, she advised against it because it would attract lots of wildlife—feeding the animals is also against Yellowstone laws. Instead, I grew some herbs in small pots that lined my kitchen windowsill—that too provided some comfort.

At home, weeding was always an annoying but necessary task. It continues to amaze me that without any help, the weeds will come. It takes great care to grow flowers and vegetables, but the weeds need no help whatsoever. What I really hate is the dang thistle that pops up everywhere. The prickly plant needs to be removed by the root and yet, somehow, it returns. I pull out two new ones along the side of the house, and even with gloves on, my finger gets pricked by one of the numerous needles. I yank off my glove and carefully pull the needle out. I'll have to remember to apply some Neosporin when I'm done, as the pricked area can get itchy.

As I bend down to resume my task, I notice a couple pieces of paper and plastic sticking to the side of the house. Irritated that people still are so lazy about putting garbage in its proper spot, I pick up the trash. I look down, and in my hand is an orange sticker. I'm suddenly paralyzed, chilled by what I see. I bring it closer to my eyes. Oh my god.

It is the stupid orange smiley face sticker from my suitcase. I look at it again, just to be sure it isn't a mirage. Holy shit. I knew Todd took my suitcase and used it in some fashion to prove my death to John. Did he miss this? It was heavily taped on. Maybe Matt removed it and it just didn't make the garbage? Who cares?!

I let out a whoop of joy, drop my gloves, and run into the house, cradling the sticker as if it were a precious stone. I'm dazed and in disbelief. I pace around, trying to find a good place for it and see my notebook. Hurriedly, I drop the sticker in the middle of it and close it, clutching it to my chest. I'm breathless at this amazing stroke of luck. Tears overcome me and I'm on my knees, thanking God.

I have my micro test.

John

In the last three days, I developed a new sense of purpose. I chucked all the alcohol, cleaned the house thoroughly, took my shirts and suits to the dry cleaners, polished and buffed my shoes, and started making repairs to the walls where I had punched holes. I replaced the broken medicine cabinet, and shopped for fresh groceries, protein supplements, and a new water filter for the refrigerator. And for the first time in months, I slept hard, without dreams, waking up invigorated.

As if a veil of darkness had been removed, I saw the dark circles under my eyes. I stepped on the scale and saw I had lost twenty pounds since Mara left. Looking at myself, naked in the mirror, I looked gaunt yet flabby. While I had still done some running, it had slowed down to maybe once every few days, and I most certainly hadn't done any weightlifting. That was all changing today.

Today I had hope again, and by God, my beloved was not going to see me at my worst. I was going to get my health back—I was going to get her back, and we are going to have our beautiful life together again. It seems a bit nutty to have this surge of belief over an orange sticker, but I just knew to the core of my being that I was going to find her.

Yesterday, I noticed that the team looked at me quizzically. I assumed that I had been walking the halls as a ghost of a human, my tragedy seeping through all my pores. Now I felt as if I was made of air, moving effortlessly, with buoyancy. A rap on my open office door woke me from my daydreaming.

"John, are you okay?" Ed asked carefully.

"Couldn't be better," I replied. But I paused a second to think. If whatever happened to Mara was on purpose, I had to be cautious of who I trusted.

"I haven't seen you this bright in months. I mean, completely understandable, given the circumstances, of, uh . . . ," He cleared his throat. ". . . of um, Mara. But did something special happen?"

"Potentially." Had to think of something plausible. "I might have met someone," I said sheepishly. I hated lying, but I realized quickly that I had to play this cool.

Ed's face brightened. "That is awesome. No disrespect, but I've been really worried about you. Obviously, I know Mara was the love of your life, and there is no deadline for grief, but I just worried about you, man."

115

The term "was" stung, but again, I now knew I needed to display an Oscar-worthy performance. "I appreciate that, really I do. I guess I just woke up one day and realized that Mara would want me to live. In an unexpected way, I met this gal. But I've only gone on one date, and I'm taking it super slow."

"I'm really happy for you, John." Ed gives me a bro hug and then goes about his day. So, shit, now that I've made that all up, I've got to figure how to keep that going as my real energy is coming from the possibility that Mara is alive. I'm going to need help, but I'll have to be spot on with who I trust.

Firing up my computer, I look at my calendar and am grateful that I don't have any meetings today or tomorrow. I can't tell my parents, most certainly, not Mara's family. Not Emile. I don't want to go back to the detective. I sit several minutes, racking my brain for the right person. Then it hits me. Jay, my sister Mallory's husband. Totally awesome dude. He and my older brother, Sean, were in the Marines together. After their tour in Iraq, Sean introduced Jay to Mallory, and it was a whirlwind romance. Their partnership is just amazing. Jay is Sean's best friend and over the years, he has become a good friend to me too. No one could have been better for wild Mallory. Mara and I have always admired their marriage and have learned much from them.

While Sean opted out of the Marines after he fulfilled his obligation and became a counselor for veterans, Jay worked his ass off and became a Navy Seal. He obviously cannot discuss his missions, but if anyone could help me put on an act, he could. I've often wondered if his alter ego is much like my favorite author Vince Flynn's beloved character, Mitch Rapp. My crazy sister is the perfect military wife—she loves Jay fiercely, and if she is ever worried when he is gone, she doesn't show it.

Everyone had tried to help before, including Jay, but we believed everything we were told. We didn't have any reason to be suspicious. But now, with a potential lead, maybe Jay would be the right person to help out. I know he isn't on assignment right now. Feeling confident, I give him a call.

"Hey, John, what's up?"

"Jay, are you free anytime this week—dinner, lunch, coffee?"

"Sure. I have a couple weeks off, as of now, until I don't." He laughs. "What's going on?"

"Would rather discuss in person, if that's okay. Can you meet me at Black Tie at six tonight?"

"Let me check with the boss. You okay?"

"Yeah great, never better," I say a little too emphatically.

He replies slowly, and I can tell he has his radar on. "Alright. I'll text you once Mal gives me the green light."

"For a badass, you definitely are whipped," I tease.

"You better believe it," he says. We hang up. Jay would do anything in the world for Mal. He had been deeply affected by Mara's disappearance, more than many, because he couldn't imagine this happening to Mal. If it was Mal, he'd use everything in his arsenal, legal or not, to find her. In this regard, I feel I let Mara down. But then I didn't have any evidence to suggest anything criminally happened. Not that I really do now, but Jay would understand my gut feeling on this.

"What's up, bro?" Jay stands up from the booth and gives me a bear hug.

"Hey, Jay. Thanks for coming to see me on short notice."

"Not a problem. Everything okay?"

Before I can answer, the server comes by and we each order a beer and a burger, though I am almost too excited to eat.

"First of all," I start, "I'm not crazy or a conspiracy theory kind of guy."

"Not at all," Jay agrees.

"So hear me out before you say anything."

"I'm all ears."

"This whole time since Mara's disappearance, weird things have been happening. Nothing that I can logically provide as tangible evidence yet, but I'll see or hear something while I'm just doing my thing, and I'll get nauseous and puke. Everything the cops and the detective have told us, I believed. But there's just something not sitting right."

Jay takes on a more serious posture. With Jay, when it is fun time, he is completely a clown, but when its business, it's all business.

"Keep talking."

After a swig of beer, I said, "I had that feeling again, and I was making myself nuts pacing around the house, so I brought out all the notes, all the reports, and all the pictures. I went through it all for hours. Nothing. Then I went to grab something in the junk drawer in the kitchen and this stupid smiley face magnet from the dentist catches my eye. I'm staring at it and it just hits me. I pull out the pictures of the suitcase that they found from the car accident. I'm staring and staring at it. I look at the magnet again, and I realize that the dumb orange sticker from Mara's suitcase isn't there."

"Okay. But a sticker could easily come off a suitcase, with it being battered around like that," he counters.

"Absolutely. Unless, of course, it was stuck on with packing tape by my anal-retentive wife."

Jay sits for a few seconds. "So you think what?"

"I don't think the suitcase in the picture is hers. The place where she etched her initials isn't in the exact right spot. It's on the inside of the handle, instead of the outside."

"Dude, I believe you. But in my line of work, where I do a lot of . . . um . . . interrogations, people who are traumatized remember whatever the captors want them to remember," he says somewhat gingerly. "Do you honestly remember it that way or could this possibly be a psychological means of getting . . ." he falters.

"Of falsely getting my hopes up?" I hit the table. "No, damnit. It's been months, how could I just drudge that up in my brain? I've checked in that luggage a thousand times. Hell, I gave her the knife to do the etching. Inside the handle would've been more difficult, which mean Mara didn't put that there."

Jay puts his hands up. "I'm totally on your side here, John." He smiles. "But now I understand why you asked me here."

"I'm sorry, I know you meant well. Why do you think you're here?"

"Because I'm awesome at what I do, and you would like to use my skill set." He grins as he takes a bite out of his burger.

I laugh. "Definitely. But it's also because you're trained to keep secrets. If I go down this path, and if you're willing to help me, no one can know, not even Mal. If I'm right and the picture isn't of her original suitcase, then someone went to great length to make us think it was." I sat silent for a second. "Which means, she got into some kind of trouble, and my god, might even be . . ."

"Alive," Jay finishes.

We stare at each other for a minute, my hand over my mouth, as I'm too frightened of jinxing this possibility by saying that word.

Suddenly, very seriously, Jay whips out his wallet, lays down fifty bucks for the thirty-five-dollar tab, and says, "Let's go back to your place." I grab my jacket, seeing him scan the room in his subtle way and out we go.

By 8 p.m., Jay and I have spread all the photos on my living room floor. I have my notebook handy, and we start brainstorming.

"We need to look at this as a 2,000-piece puzzle," he says. "You know how people generally start with the corners, then the edges, then start grouping by the distinct colors and images and leave the blurry or same colored ones, like blue sky, for last? That's how we are going to look at this. I really wish you had one of those big whiteboards we could draw or tape on."

"Help me move the sofa out of the way. I have tons of 36x48 old blueprints that we can tape together on the wall—we can draw on the back of them. I'll go grab some out of the basement while you grab us another beer," I instruct.

We take the time to tape eight sheets to the now bare wall, and I pull out a couple of markers from my office.

"Let's start with four corners, these are the four fundamental things we know that will be the foundation for the rest of it," Jay says. It's kind of fun watching him move into his tactical and strategic self.

"Let's start with why Mara left in the first place—to do some sort of undercover story, right?"

"She got a big lead from one of her very reliable sources about a sex trafficking ring out West, something that could upset a lot of people in power, is all I know."

"What makes you think she went west?"

"I saw some of the stuff she was packing. No designer outfits or heels. Several of her jeans and flannel shirts aren't in the closet, so she isn't going as far as California. And the pictures of the cliff she supposedly went off had mountains in the background and the lighting that's only present in areas like Colorado, Idaho, Montana, and Wyoming. That and it was Colorado cops who talked to me on the phone and one came out with a Colorado badge."

"Are you feeling that everything was in Colorado?" he asks.

"That's the only indication we have so far."

"But we're going to have to think like Sherlock. You know, whatever is probable is possible."

"Agreed. Mara seemed confident about where she was going, she didn't appear to be concerned about navigating it."

"What did she have to drive?"

I pull out the picture of the really nice black Jeep, well, what used to be a nice Jeep. It's on its back like a bug with the one side crunched together like a squashed tin can. The wheels are heavy and industrial, made for terrain driving.

"No doubt this model had a good GPS on it," Jay says admiringly. "Did the cops or the detective you hired go through the GPS logs on it?"

I think about that for a minute. "I don't recall either saying anything about it, maybe it says something in the report. Hard to believe I would miss anything, as I've read that damn thing a million times."

I scan through it and hand it to Jay for a second perusal. "It's odd that it isn't mentioned in here. It's now a standard thing for accidents, especially for ones that could be considered irregular. Kinda like the black box in an airplane. Do you still have the contact information for the police who brought the news and the detective?"

I nodded. I had called the detective a few times after he went through his findings with me. I would think of something that maybe didn't get addressed and he'd tell me that a) it wasn't possible or b) it was already covered as a result of the details already in the report. And every time, more grains of hope slipped through the hourglass.

"How did I miss asking him or the cops about that?" I angrily shake my head. "I'm a freaking idiot."

"Dude, no one thinks crystal clear in a stressful situation they haven't trained for—even in my line of work, we have to do constant scenario training just to keep that from happening. A regular guy like you isn't going to think that way, so don't beat yourself up over it." He puts my hand on my shoulder as he heads to the kitchen for another beer.

"Okay, last one for the night and then I need to get home or the kids will be pissed I missed them before bed. Put that on your to-do list—call the cops and call the detective and ask about the GPS logs."

Jotting it in the notebook, I ask, "So let's say they tell me there aren't any?"

"Bullshit. With a vehicle like that, it most certainly has it because of these adventurous types who can't tell north and south. It's one the best features for weekend warriors. If they tell you there aren't any, they're lying."

We both pause to think about that.

"My God. Is it possible that they're lying? And to what end?"

Jay slugs down one more gulp. "Brother, if Mara was going there to look into a high-level trafficking thing and they are lying, we have big problems."

After confirming that Jay is good to drive home, I rinse out the beer bottles, tossing them into the recycling bin. There's that strange feeling in my gut again. The only thing going through my head is what if they are lying? It opens a whole different door. And it frightens me. It frightens me enough to churn my stomach and I go puke again. I slump on the floor against the cool steps that go up to the platform jacuzzi tub.

Sitting with my head in my hands, to help stave off another round of vomiting, I try to focus. But I can't. The idea that something afoul is at hand presses heavily on my chest. My anxiety and fear turn to anger, anger at myself that this stupid GPS thing could have been figured out months ago. What a colossal waste of time. What if my wasting time caused Mara harm? Damnit, she could be here RIGHT NOW! I pound my hand against the pearl-gray floor tile. I take a breath and get up. I am not going to break anything, I tell myself, crazy frustrated as I am.

I hear my mother's soothing voice in my head, "John, regret is a scab—you either keep opening it up or you let it heal. The scar that comes after reminds you not to make the same mistake again." I know she's right, but I'm not good at being powerless. Screw it. I'm going to brush my teeth, go to bed, and call these jerks tomorrow morning. I don't know how Jay leads a normal life—able to turn the shit he has seen and had to do off when he is at home. He is going to need to teach me to be more levelheaded, or I'll end up missing something else.

Mara

Since I found the sticker, I can think of little else. But I must keep my cool. I need to think about printing the right labels on the coffee bean bags. The roasters require checking every hour. Invoices need to get out to our larger clients and the credit cards must be run for the online purchases. That has been the latest development—an online presence. Seems that many of the tourists who bought coffee at any of the Yellowstone shops have contacted us for individual purchases.

Damon couldn't be happier. Of course, we now have a deluxe, professional espresso machine hooked up here for our benefit. Once in a while, after a trip to South America, Damon will bring in new beans to experiment with, to broaden our collection. Naturally, we do tastings, a definite benefit of the job. Occasionally, Damon will disassemble the machine to take to clients for demonstration of the new fresh beans. I am now so spoiled with having it here, I'm bereft when it is gone.

He is here today and brings me a fresh cup with creamer in it, with a mug in his own hand. "Good morning. Can we make time to review this month's sales and accounts receivable later this morning? I have the quarterly meeting with the CPA on Friday."

"Not a problem. I just need a couple hours to get a few things done. Would eleven work?"

"Perfect. I'm going to run to the hardware store for this project Emma has for me at the house. Actually, I'm having a couple of guys do the work, but I thought I better buy the materials myself. Not that I don't trust them, but it's just better if I do it."

I stifle a giggle. "Because you're a closet control freak?"

"Oh no, I'm a fully outed control freak, if you haven't figured out," he says cheekily.

"What's Emma up to today?"

"She and the kids are driving to Bozeman to this natural science museum and this history thing as part of their assignments for this term. I got to hand it to her, she is amazing at figuring how to take one subject and make assignments for all of them at their level. I could never do it."

I respond while rolling my eyes, "That's because you are too hyper."

He laughs. "True. Why are you being so mean today? I remembered the creamer this time."

"Me? Mean? C'mon, I'm lovable Anne, remember? I just woke up today feeling really good about things, nothing in particular."

"Well, cool. Hopefully, the stuff you give me for the CPA will make me as buoyant."

"Guaranteed," I reply. We are doing well. Every month that we are up, I get a $500 bonus. Not that I need the money, but it is nice to be appreciated. I become temporarily melancholy when I think that this too will end. I have absolutely no clue how I'm going to tell him.

After I finish giving Damon the reports he needs for his visit with the CPA, I go through my daily checklist to see if I have forgotten anything. Confirming completion, I set upon another task: how to communicate to John that I am alive, where I am at, and how to warn him to be careful.

It is too risky to send a package or a note to his office or to our house. I don't even want to risk sending anything to anyone in our families. Can't send to Ron, at my office. What about places that John frequents? The gym? Too removed and greater risk the package wouldn't get to him. Emile and Victoria? Definitely not. They would want him to open it right then and there, nosy and lovable as they are. Most certainly not the Black Tie, where we are regulars for after-work gatherings with friends and family. *Think, Mara, think!*

But just like how one cannot retrace steps initially when losing keys, I'm having a brain block. The harder one thinks, the more elusive the answer becomes. I need to do something mindless to overcome it. Moving back to the computer, I pull up email and check for orders. Two more today. Awesome! After confirming the orders and processing the credit cards, I print out the labels and box them up for UPS to pick up this afternoon.

Oh my god! It. Is. Right. Under. My. Nose. I'll mail a sampler to my friend Jill Mayer at Espresso Yourself! She gets samplers from roasters all the time. As ideas are pouring into my brain, I make myself stop. I need to make a list of the pros and cons of everything. It is imperative I don't rush into this and make a fatal error.

Todd knows about Espresso Yourself, but after this much time, he probably won't be watching it as frequently. I'm betting that John still goes there two to three times a week.

What about the return address? While Jill won't think anything about it, if John is under surveillance and makes any connection, his expression could alert Todd. How do I put something in there for John that won't stir up Jill? I could see her trying to figure out why there is something for John in her box, flipping out, calling him all excited, and thus alerting Todd. I'm going to have to be less direct, but this is going to take time to cook up and Damon will be back soon. Not that I want to hide anything from him, but I must, for now.

John

When I call the Colorado policeman's number that was given to me, the message on the phone said, "This line is no longer in service." I start shaking. It takes me a minute, but I try the number two more times in case I may have dialed incorrectly the first time. I jot this down in the notebook, as now I have become a little more paranoid about saying anything to Jay over the phone or via email. Even more so now, with this discovery.

Getting my nerve back, I call private detective Joel Crane's number and get the same kind of message. I get on the internet and search the phone number via white pages—nothing. I enter the address on the card and try to use Google Maps to see where this address on the business card is located. I am presented with what looks to be a condemned building. Damn it! Who gave me the referral in the first place? Shit! It was Ed. My partner. My friend. What the hell?

Confusion overtakes me. How could Ed be so careless as to give me a bogus, dead end referral? He saw my grief. He knows that Mara's disappearance has been tearing me apart. Has he even met Joel Crane? My confusion slowly turns to clarity then to anger. Is he purposely misleading me? Is he involved in Mara's disappearance? Has he been hiding behind this facade the entire time? What did we ever do to him? Why? I have so many questions.

My head is spinning so hard that the bile of deceit comes quickly up my throat, and I barely make it to the bathroom. My stomach muscles hurt from all the retching, created by fury and disbelief occupying the same space.

My watch says it is almost 8 a.m., almost time to go to the office to confront the son of a bitch. I'm utterly convinced that something has gone terribly wrong. I need to talk to Jay before I go in or else I may do something illegal, or at least something I will regret.

I text Jay, "Can you meet me at Espresso Yourself?"

"I can be there in 20 mins after I drop off kids at school," he replies.

"Thx."

We arrive at about the same time, and I tell Jay about this morning's discoveries. He agrees that things are not kosher.

"Okay, John, you will have to keep your cool here. I know you're pissed, but we need information. We don't want to spook him into doing something."

"I can't promise that."

"You're going to have to. Remember the greater good, the big picture—getting us closer to the truth about Mara."

"Can I hit him?" I ask half kidding, half serious.

"No. I'll go with you."

"Fine."

We drive to the office separately. As we are about to walk to the front entrance, Jay reaffirms, "Do not hit him."

I roll my eyes. Though I'm appreciative of his presence. I smile politely at Jenna, our receptionist, and ask, "Is Ed in his office?"

"You caught him at a good time, no meetings for another two hours."

"Great, thanks."

The door to Ed's office is open, he stands and smiles at seeing Jay. "Hey stranger, good to see you," he says, extending his arm for a handshake. Bastard. Jay takes it and puts forth a little small talk, thus restraining me from going all in. After a few minutes, he leads me in, as he shuts Ed's door. "Ed, we actually came together with a purpose."

"Go ahead."

I start slowly, saying, "It appears that everything we were given, regarding Mara, is proving false."

No micro expression yet, in fact, he eyes widen. "Are you serious? My God, after all this time? Good news, I hope?"

Jay and I exchange glances, then Jay replies, "How did you come to know the detective, Joel Crane, who you referred to John?"

Without a beat to think of a lie he answers, "He's the husband of a client of mine. We did a remodel of her family's store in Plymouth a couple of years ago. I remembered her telling me that her husband is a private investigator and gave the information to you."

My voice remains measured, but I'm sure my expression is dark and accusatory, "Funny. I was reviewing some notes the other day, and something wasn't jiving, so I called him. I got a message that his number had been disconnected. I searched the address on his card and it seems it is an abandoned warehouse."

I pause to let it all sink in. To let him come to the realization that I know he's involved in Mara's disappearance. I want to see the fear in his eyes. "So you can imagine what I'm thinking . . ."

He stands up slowly as things start to click. "For God's sake! You think I had something to do with this? Have you lost your mind?" he says angrily.

"Good ploy, move to offense," Jay retorts. "Yes, you can see how we think you're involved."

"How could I possibly know? I never even met this guy. Is this what twenty-plus years of friendship means?"

"Screw you!" I exclaim, getting in his face. "Not ever have Mara or I done anything to you to deserve this. You are one of my family. How could you betray and watch me die like this?"

Ed is visibly shaking, and his voice elevates in both tone and volume, "John, I am telling you the truth. When I knew you were looking for an investigator, I thought of him. His wife is a freaking angel. I can't believe she'd be married to some criminal."

"Guess we're all in disbelief," I say sarcastically.

Ed sits back at his computer and begins typing frantically. "Here. Here is her name, number, and the address of the shop. Go talk to her. I have nothing to hide. Mara is my friend too—I would never cause her harm."

Not ready to believe him yet, I say, "Too late."

Jay steps in, "John, let's give the man the benefit of the doubt. What would he gain from seeing you in this much pain?"

I mull it over, sinking into the chair, and utter softly, "Nothing."

Ed jumps up. "John, I swear to you, if something bad has happened, I'll do whatever you need to help find the answers. Seriously."

I can't help myself, but tears form in my eyes. "I'm sorry. I should've known better."

Ed shakes it off. "Hey, I would be the same way. I'm just glad you didn't start with ripping my head off. We'll get to the bottom of this," he says with a reaffirming hand on my shoulder. He and Jay shake hands again, and Ed asks, "What can I do?"

Jay answers, "You do nothing right now. You don't say anything to anyone, including your wife. Try to act like nothing happened here today. Watch what you email, what you say, who you talk to. We're going to go pay the wife a visit. I'll text you when we have the next steps, but I cannot emphasize this enough: something has gone wrong, and it is very possible this office, John's house, or other places are being watched. Be normal but be careful."

Jay looks at the sheet, and says, "I know this place. I get a lot of my gear there. Small world."

We then leave Ed's office, throwing the sheet into the recycling bin.

Jay and I decide to leave my car at my house and take his to Mrs. Crane's store in Plymouth, a 20-minute drive from here. As Jay drives with one hand, he has the forefinger of his other hand over his mouth, his thumb under his chin, leaning on the armrest, deep in thought. After a few minutes, he breaks the silence.

"John, I have until two o'clock today to go wherever this takes us. I want you to realize this may lead us nowhere and there might be a less evil reason for all of this."

"I can hardly think of any," I reply, mystified.

"Hear me out. There's one possibility I know you haven't expressed at all."

"What?"

He takes his eyes off the road, looking hard into mine. "There is the possibility that Mara may not have wanted to be found. That for some unknown reason, she chose to disappear . . . that she left . . . you."

I instantly blow up, "Fuck you and go to hell! How can you even say that?"

"Because I'm trained to deal with hard, impossible-to-believe, cold truths. You owe it to yourself to consider this possibility."

"Screw your job, this is Mara, not some damn ISIS terrorist you're interrogating."

Jay pauses, then continues, "That's true. But as much as we know anyone, we never can fully know what is in their heads. I'm just asking you to consider it."

"Do you think like that when it comes to Mal?" I say, hoping to press his buttons so he too can feel the sting I'm reeling from.

"I am a cold-blooded realist. I've learned to assume nothing, which is why I'm grateful every day I wake up next to that woman or hear her voice on the phone. She would have more reasons to leave me than I think Mara would have to leave you. I'm simply trying to point out all scenarios that come to mind."

I am still agitated. "Let's leave that one for last. Crazy as it sounds, I could somehow accept if she were dead, but if she left me, I'd truly shrivel up and die. If she cooked up something this spectacular to leave me, the only conclusion I can take from that is that I must be some kind of monster."

Jay smiles. "And we all know you are not a monster. Just remember I'm your ally, not your enemy. Allies put it all on the table."

"I know, it just stung like hell to hear you say it because truth is, it has crossed my mind several times."

"It would take Mara weeks or months to put together an elaborate plan like this. People are easier to find than one thinks, especially Westerners."

"You saying my girl isn't smart enough?" I jab at him.

"Didn't say that at all, but trained as she is to keep secrets, doing so for a long time is difficult." I nod in agreement and point out that we have arrived.

The store, Al's Outfitters, is in the middle of one of the many countless retail strips in the city. Nestled in between a posh-looking Thai restaurant and an eclectic consignment book store. As we look around the various camouflage and desert gear, a sales clerk approaches us, asking if we need assistance.

Jay answers, "I'm a personal client of Julia Stein—is she here today?"

The sales clerk, obviously bedazzled by hunky Jay, replies, "Of course, sir, who can I tell her is here?"

"Jay Ramierez." She flashes him a smile and quickly darts for the office, probably to conceal her girlish blush.

I roll my eyes. "You are a piece of work."

He laughs. "Charm to disarm. Nice stuff you're looking at. That wicked jagged knife? That is a Lucifer Bowie Damascus steel knife; 256 layers of steel and about $300. Oh, and look at that beauty." He points to a black straight edge. "That is the Benchmade Foray. Gorgeous black carbon fiber handle. That bitch can cut through a ripe tomato or someone's finger quite aptly."

"You scare me at times."

He lifts his eyebrows, doing his Joker impression. "And I should." He laughs manically.

"I see you are drooling on my showcase again," says the voice behind us.

We both turn around to see a stunning woman. She appears Eurasian with her almond black eyes and honey colored hair. She and Jay exchange pecks on both cheeks, and she extends a hand to me. "I'm Julia Stein."

"Julia, a pleasure, I'm John Finegan. Obviously, you know my brother-in-law Jay."

"Jay has been a client for a long time, but he never said he had an equally handsome brother-in-law. Are you in the same line of work?"

Trying to overcome my blushing, I say, "No, I'm a boring

engineering and architecture guy. In fact, my partner, Ed Mansfield, is the one who did the remodel of this store."

"What a small world!" Julia exclaims. "A lovely job he did."

"Thank you, but there is about to be another coincidence."

Jay puts the pieces together. "John is the husband of Mara Riley-Finegan, the reporter from the Trib."

It takes her a minute, but when she places the name, she says, "Oh goodness. I am so sorry for your loss. I loved reading her articles. Brilliant journalist. But I guess I'm not understanding the connection to me and the store?"

"It is about your husband, Joel."

Her expression goes dark. "What's going on here, Jay?"

Jay explains that Ed gave Joel's name to me to help in the investigation of Mara's disappearance. She shakes her head. "Well, maybe you can help me find Joel." We both look at her quizzically, as she continues, "Joel got really wound up several months ago. Said he had to disappear or there would be trouble for us. That he did something stupid and he couldn't go to the police. All I know is that he's in Chicago. He calls sporadically to talk to the kids—five minutes at a time. I can't get him to tell me anything, I can't get him to go to the police or come home. But I'm scared for him, for us, and I'm angry, wondering what the hell he got himself into."

"How do you know he's in Chicago?" Jay asks.

"Even though I know he is using burner phones, they always have a Chicago area code—that's what shows up on my phone and I just quick checked it. He puts money in our account through some non-bank app—I'm hoping it isn't illegal money."

"Have you gone to the police?"

"No, I'm too scared and I don't want to worry the kids. He assures me that unless more than a week goes by without hearing from him, he is safe. I just tell the kids Daddy is on an assignment. But what kind of marriage is this?" she says as tears start coming down her face.

"Julia, do you trust me?" Jay replies, holding both of her shoulders and squatting to meet her gaze.

"Yes."

"Okay, we are just at the beginning of this, but John and I think that Mara didn't die in some random accident. We're not even convinced she's dead. I think if we can help Joel, we'll get some answers about Mara."

She nods and vigorously wipes away the tears. "That would be so kind of you. Thank you, Jay, thank you both." She takes my hand.

"I hope it helps you too."

Back in the car, Jay said, "Give me a few days to work with some buddies of mine at Chicago PD. They'll know what to do."

"Yeah, but he uses burner phones, how do you trace them?"

"There's a chance, professional or not, that in an emotional state, the detective forgot to remove the SIM card from the burners. If we get that lucky, they can pinpoint where the last call was made and trace it to the place where he bought it. More than likely, wherever those two places are, they are in close proximity. People in distress don't have the discipline to make those two places as far apart as possible."

"I need to watch more TV," I say.

Jay rolls his eyes. "Glad your humor is back."

A couple of days after our meeting with Julia Stein, I'm at the office trying to work on specs for a client, but I'm finding it difficult to concentrate. I relayed our findings to Ed and apologized again for jumping down his throat.

"Stop it already. We're good, I would have reacted the same way. I can't believe there is more to this—it's so surreal. Just let me know what you need me to do."

"Thank you, for everything."

Shortly after, Jay calls, "Dude, my buddies were able to circle in and after showing Ed's picture, they freaking found him."

"No shit! Are you kidding? When do we go to Chicago?"

"We aren't going anywhere. Modern technology is going to take over. They have him at their station, and we are going to have a teleconference."

"When?" I ask excitedly.

"In about two hours. My buddy had to get it cleared with his boss, yada, yada. I'm coming to you, but give me your Skype info so I can give it to them."

I give him the info and then start pacing, unable to concentrate on anything. I call in one of the junior partners and ask if she can take the job I was working on. She's a good kid, she'll do fine.

Meanwhile, to pass the time, I run to get a sandwich and a coffee at Espresso Yourself. Jill greets me and starts preparing my Americano with a double shot. She says, "Hey, John, I'll have yours up in a minute. I'm trying out a sampler from a roaster I'm not familiar with. But a pound of free beans is still free beans. Okay being my guinea pig?"

I barely hear the question, and distractedly reply, "Yeah, sure. No problem."

She hands me my drink and, as I head out toward the door, she calls out, "John, hey, sorry, one more thing."

I quickly walk back, though I'm anxious to return to my office. "What's up?"

"Inside the box from the roaster was five survey cards. I'm supposed to give them to my favorite customers. You fill it out, send it back to them, and then they send me a five-pound bag of beans for free. If I buy twenty pounds a month, I'll get 30 percent off each time." She smiles at me sweetly. "I know you want to help your favorite barista."

"Okay, sure." I stuff the card in my pocket and head back to work.

Jay and Ed join me in my office to talk to Detective Joel Crane. The guy is supposedly thirty-eight years old, but he looks 20 years older. I look at the printout picture we have and look at the screen. It is astonishing what stress does to a person. I should talk. I haven't gotten back to my former self yet, but I'm looking better than I did a couple weeks ago. Maybe it isn't a fountain of youth people should strive for but an inkling of hope.

A gravelly voice starts speaking, "Hold on, Jay." It matches a chiseled face. "I need to get a separate camera on this."

"Thanks, Captain, I appreciate your help on this unorthodox mission."

"No problem. We can't keep this guy here forever, so let's get rolling."

Jay had told me that Captain Zeller was part of his platoon in the Marines and he knows my brother, Sean, as well, which made the request easier to grant. The camera shifts to Joel. Zeller had Jay provide a list of questions we needed answered—he had his own way of questioning, which required us to relinquish this interview to him. I was fine with that, as I didn't want to lose control and scare the guy into clamming up.

"How did you come to get involved with the Mara Riley-Finegan case?" Zeller started.

"My wife gave Ed my name. I found out Ed and Mara's husband, John Finegan, are business partners," he said, making eye contact through the camera.

"So it was just circumstance or coincidence that you got involved?"

"Special circumstance."

Zeller is now inching closer, planting himself on the corner of the table Crane is sitting at. "Keep going. The more forthright you are without me having to ask particular questions, the better off you will be."

Crane looks down at his lap, you can tell his mind is churning, thinking about the best way to move forward. Jay, Ed, and I simultaneously, unconsciously, move closer to the screen. "The guy on the right, that's Ed who worked on my wife's family store. I had looked up the firm when he had made his first bid and saw John Finegan, the guy in the middle. I didn't think anything of it at the time."

His eyes were imploring us as he continues, "Ed was at the store presenting my wife with a final draft of the remodel and there was a newspaper on the counter with the picture and a headline about Mara Riley-Finegan, the journalist, going missing."

I cringe. That front page is seared in my brain forever—I provided the picture for Ron, Mara's editor, to use. "I had read the article and then remembered that Ed's partner was Mara's husband. I had told my wife about it and suggested she introduce me to Ed, as I wished to help. I knew my wife followed Mara's work."

I start to open my mouth, wanting to ask why he bullshit me, why didn't he want to tell me the truth from the start. Jay must have telepathic power because out of my peripheral vision, I could see him shaking his head no at me.

"I never wanted anything bad to happen," Crane says.

"You're doing great, keep going," Zeller encourages.

"A month after John hired me, a man hacked me on my computer and told me I needed to botch the investigation. Long story short, he has something on me that would hurt my wife and kids, and I'd never be able to work as an investigator again." He stopped for a few seconds. "He said if I went to the police he would carry out his threat."

"There are always ways around stuff like this. It's a tactic. Besides, if the idiot was stupid enough to hack you, he's got his own troubles to contend with," Zeller returned.

"There's more. I was stupid enough to accept $200k from this guy, who put it in an off-shore account."

"You are stupid," Zeller agreed. "If the guy can put it in, he can remove it. Did you withdraw any of it?"

"From time to time I put money in our savings account so Julie wouldn't think I had left her and the kids high and dry."

"For an investigator, you're pretty freaking naive," Zeller barked. "Why would you simply believe this guy?"

"Because he provided evidence of my sins."

Zeller yelled, "I don't give a damn about your sins, I need to know what happened to Mara Riley-Finegan!"

"Just because I provided false information to John doesn't mean I know the truth," Crane countered.

Switching gears, Zeller asked, "Did you meet this person? What about phone calls, email, regular mail, how did you stay in contact?"

"All I know is his name, or at least what he said his name was: Eric."

"No last name?"

"I doubt a guy who hacks computers is going to give out his last name," Crane replied dryly.

Everyone paused for a moment. I moved away from the computer. "We aren't getting any closer than where we were before."

Jay motioned me back. "C'mon John, you can do this."

Zeller looked at us. "John, can you think of anyone in Mara's life with the name Eric?"

I rattled my brain, but I couldn't think of anyone. "Think, John, think," I told myself, but to no avail, and I shook my head no.

"Crane, is there anything else?"

"Honest to God, no. But I've cooperated and risked Eric coming through on his threat. What are you going to do to help me?"

Zeller answered, "We have some pretty good hackers ourselves. We'll get rid of your 'sins.' After you send John what he paid you to help find his wife, you'll anonymously send the majority of the money you got to a charity of my choice. Then you get out of the investigating business, find a boring nine-to-five job, and get good with your kids and old lady."

To us, Zeller asked, "Anything else you need?" We shook our heads, offered our thanks, and signed off. I said to Jay and Ed, "Maybe I can check with Ron Edwards, Mara's editor. Maybe he knows someone she's done a story with or a source named Eric."

"I'm concerned about letting another person in on this whole thing. Every time we do, we expose ourselves exponentially," Jay cautioned.

"Throughout the interview, it made me wonder how this Eric person would have known to hack into Joel's computer? I have to believe the office, me, John, and John's house must be under surveillance," Ed speculated.

"I totally agree with you," Jay said. "Luckily, even if this Eric guy was looking to spy on me, he wouldn't be able to hack into my computer. Let's assume this is the case. On your phones, you'll need to change your passwords to all critical accounts, banks, social media, etc. and then try to stay off those apps on any desktop computer. I'll get you guys some external drives to download crucial business and client records, then we'll get some heavily protected laptops for you both."

"But if this guy is watching us, wouldn't it alert him if we suddenly stopped certain electronic activities?" I asked.

"Good point. Just change your passwords to all financial accounts."

"How are we going to keep him from knowing what we're doing without alarms going off?" Ed asked.

"We need some kind of decoy," Jay answered. We all sat there for several minutes without any of us coming up with any ideas.

Mara

"Hey, Damon, I got my first response," I announced, poking my head into his office.

"That's cool! I'm curious to see how this experiment pans out."

I had told Damon my idea, after I already shipped out the box to Jill. I didn't want to risk him saying no. As Damon is a guy born for marketing, I felt confident he would go for it. The idea was to send enough juju to Jill to get her to give a card to John. It was super subtle, but when I designed the cards, I placed an orange smiley face on the back of each one. It wouldn't mean anything to anyone else, but John teased me enough about it that if he saw it, he would have to know it was me trying to reach him.

If John sent it back, I could send a less subtle message with the free beans—even if none of the other four cards came back—when John's arrived, I would. The card that was returned, to my disappointment, was from Mary Jean, Jill's younger sister, which also made me laugh. I suppose I didn't make any rules regarding family. However, it had been two weeks and I was getting impatient.

"Anne, if it was sent out two weeks ago, that's hardly any time for shipping both ways—I was honestly surprised and excited to see this first card already," Damon calmly countered my pique.

"I know, I know. I did send out another box to a place in Santa Cruz that I had been to before. I remember the people there were really cool. And it is a great touristy site."

"Yes, it is. I'm from San Francisco—Santa Cruz is a great area to take the kids. Awesome amusement park on the Boardwalk. Good choice."

Trying to be nonchalant, I said, "Any other particular market you'd like me to try?'

"This first one to Minneapolis is fine, but let's stick to the West Coast for now. Let's see what you can find in the Pike's Place neighborhood in Seattle. I realize it goes against mighty Starbucks and Seattle's Best, but Seattle always has room for another organic roaster."

I saluted, and said, "You got it, boss." I was happy to have another assignment to keep my mind off things.

Later, when I got home (I still despise saying that word, knowing it means here and not there), I decided to run through the small accumulating pile of meaningless ads, flyers, and so on. Then there was that horrible priority envelope, indicating that Todd had sent me something. Instead of the usual dread, I was actually anxious to open it this time.

There were several pictures of John and what looked like a woman coming out of my house. What the hell? One photo even showed them intensely kissing, her in my goddamn blue robe! Oh my God. No. No. NO! I couldn't look at the rest. The letter read:

Dear Mara,

I was getting a little bored with John's moping about. Couldn't believe he was still mourning you. I had stopped watching him daily, as it was so tedious, and then just the other day, this gem happened. She is pretty, and they seem fairly enamored with each other, and I would guess, deep in sin. Very clear that he has forgotten his marriage vows to you.

You know, Mara, if this gets serious enough, they may even get married. After of course, John FINALLY declares you dead. Once that happens, you wouldn't have any claim to property or to him. And I can't imagine you so heartless as to selfishly insert yourself back into his life. Maybe I'll consider lifting the ban. It would be quite juicy to see his anguish of not waiting longer.

Or not. Don't do anything foolish, Mara. I will take him out, as promised, if you try to contact him.

With Love,

Todd

I screamed at the top of my lungs in frustration. I was so close to getting in contact with John. I have been so careful and patient. Why, God, WHY?! I ripped the note to shreds and was about to rip up the photos. Deciding I was a glutton for punishment, I looked at them again closer, wiping away the tears. I couldn't see the woman's face in the first few. The fourth one, I could, and I looked hard. Better not be someone I know.

Huh?

No way. It was Jay's sister, Chelsey. Chelsey, who was in a deeply committed relationship to Olivia.

Chelsey, an actress.

John

It's been over a year since I kissed Mara, or any other woman for that matter. But I needed to be convincing. Jay and I had a conversation with Chelsey, Olivia, and my crazy sister, Mallory. I didn't want there to be an issue with keeping secrets from Mal, and she would keep her word about keeping this from the two families. Also, she can come up with some whacked out ideas and this one was hers. She, Chelsey, and Olivia are a scary group—I would pit them against Jay and his crew any day.

It was the three of them who came up with the idea of having Chelsey pretend to be my new girlfriend.

"Geesh, Mal, that is truly like kissing . . . I don't know . . . like kissing you! I can't do this, and I can't ask Olivia to be okay with it," I exclaimed.

"Olivia is sitting right here," Olivia bantered in third person. "My sweetie is an actress, and to keep an income coming, she's had to kiss lots of men. It isn't sex or anything, just business."

"You sound like you're whoring me out," Chelsey laughed. "But seriously, if this means getting our Mara back, I'd freaking kiss a Southern preacher. No biggie. But we're going to have to practice," she teased.

"Why do I still feel like it would be incestual?"

"Because you're a prude and have had only, mmm . . . how many lovers in your life?" Mallory goaded.

"Just because you were a slut doesn't mean I was," I retorted, half kidding.

"Dude, that's my bride you are talking about," Jay said, adding into this nonsense.

"Seriously, John. I don't have cooties, but to be convincing we are going to have to practice this," Chelsey said.

"It isn't that at all, you pain in the ass. It feels . . ." I paused, groping for the right word. " . . . It feels disloyal."

The girls sigh simultaneously. "John, we're here to help. It is about Mara, right?" Mal countered.

"Right, and thank you for wanting to help. But it is imperative this doesn't get out to anyone. I feel this jackass is watching the house, my office, and who knows where else."

"We get it." Mal smiled as she cleared away several beer bottles.

"No time like the present. Stand up, big boy, and plant one on me," beckoned Chelsey.

"What, like now?"

"Yes, now." She yanked me out of my chair, and before I knew it my head was in her hands and her open lips were on my surprised ones. My face had to be turning fifty shades of red.

"Not bad, but you are out of practice. Just relax. Now, kiss me." Jay barked, "John, kiss the woman!"

I gritted my teeth and bared down, leaning over, trying to figure out an appropriate place for my hands. She gently grabbed them and put them around her waist. I concentrated on relaxing, pretending it was Mara, and ever so gently kissed her.

Olivia nodded approvingly, "Much better, that was real."

"Because he was thinking of Mara," Chelsey smiled. "I don't enjoy kissing my fellow male actors, but I do the same thing, I think of Olivia."

"It helped. But now that we've high schooled this thing, it's necessary to concoct a means for this Eric guy to see it," I said.

John

In all honesty, I was grateful to have "practiced" with Chelsey before staging a sincere, passionate kiss for Eric to get a snapshot. It was the one time I hoped that he was watching. It made me angry to think that my privacy has been invaded, not that I was doing much these last several months except mourning.

But now I felt like I had a greater purpose, a reason to hope again. I allowed myself to think about Mara. To wake and pretend she was next to me—her hair a tangled heap, smiling at me with warm eyes—made getting up for the day easier. Hope is a powerful force. It can get one through the toughest of times, or it can lead you to a path of denial so deep you can't recover. After all this time, I was going to believe in the first.

Part of keeping myself in check was to keep the routines in place. In the last few weeks, I had got back to going for a run nearly every day. I had forced myself to really tune in to my work. I was eating better and cutting back on the booze. Shifting into park, I also was keeping another routine—grabbing a coffee at Espresso Yourself.

"Hey, John," Jill waved from behind the counter. "We'll have your Americano up in a jiff."

"Good morning. How about one of those fresh squeezed OJs as well?"

"Absolutely. But I do have a bone to pick with you."

I was a little shocked—rarely did I encounter Jill with anything but bubbly enthusiasm. "What did I do?"

"It's what you haven't done yet," she said, glaring over her thick purple-framed glasses. "I haven't gotten my free coffee yet because somebody hasn't sent in their card."

I had to think for a minute. "Oh right, the survey." I held up my hands in surrender. "It's probably in one of my pockets or on my desk. I'll find it and get it done, I promise."

"You better or there won't be special treatment for you. Other customers got it done and like this brand. If you are keeping me from future sales . . . well . . ."

"I got it. I promise I'll do it. See? I'm putting a reminder in my phone right now."

She handed me my drinks, and I gave her a charming smile and put an extra couple bucks in the tip jar.

"I'm serious, John. Your two bucks only buys you so much cred here," she said, feigning indignation.

I walked out and made my way to the office. Coffee, good god. Why are we such slaves? But I knew I better keep my promise. Just because five pounds of coffee was irrelevant to me didn't give me the right to not take her seriously. It really is good coffee.

Happy to be home after a long but truly productive day, I got out of my dress shirt and slacks and slipped into a pair of shorts and a T-shirt. I went to the fridge to fill my water bottle with ice and filtered water. That was another thing, drinking more water kept me from getting lethargic, and just started tasting better. It became important to me to be in shape, for what I didn't know exactly. But something in me said to prepare for whatever may happen. I hadn't thrown up in weeks, I wasn't getting the shakes anymore, and the bouts of oppressive sadness were lifting. It felt like the elephant was finally getting off my chest.

As I made my way to the living room, I felt my phone vibrating in my pocket. It was the reminder to look for that survey card for Jill. Ugh, I just wanted to sit with my laptop, pay the bills, and then relinquish myself to tonight's football game. But a promise is a promise. I headed to the bedroom and starting rummaging through the pockets of sport jackets and dress slacks, nothing there. I didn't think there would be because, as a creature of habit, I empty out my pockets in the office first and then get changed.

I went back to my home office, saw my wallet, my keys, and my computer bag. But I didn't see a card. I lifted a couple of files, moved the keyboard, and opened the two drawers but didn't see anything. I was about to give up, when I spotted a card on the floor by my desk chair. I'm not sure how I didn't see it when I was vacuuming a couple of days ago, but there it was. I scanned the top and saw the address was out of Montana. That's cool. I love that place, but I don't remember it at all from the last time Mara and I were there. I filled out the questions quickly, saw that it was prestamped, and put it on top of my computer bag so I would remember to put it in our mailbox for outgoing mail.

And then I turned it over. The breath rushed out of my lungs in a single gasp. I sank into the chair just as the shaking and nausea began. My brain is screaming at me, "No fucking way. My god, Mara is alive. She is ALIVE." I glanced dizzyingly at the stupid orange smiley face in the corner of the card for a second time. I rushed to the bathroom to throw up.

Recovering from that, I became a wind-up toy without direction. I paced around, trying to get myself under control. I mean, it had to be from Mara. I looked at the card again. There was nothing in the logo that would tie it to the orange sticker. Obviously, it wasn't 100-percent proof, but my god, it couldn't just be coincidence either. Do I call Jay? No. That could tip off this Eric guy. Do I call the Roastery in Montana? Even worse idea. Don't know if it be problematic for Mara. What the hell do I do?

I took a few breaths, ate a couple of crackers, drank some more water, and brushed my teeth to get rid of that nasty bile taste. I also needed to calm myself in order to make a good decision. I decided a cryptic text to Jay would be safe.

"Hey, want to go grab a beer?"

"Sure, but it will have to be just one, after 8 pm. We have a parent-teacher conference to go to."

"Okay, meet you at Black Tie then."

I texted the same request to Ed, who was also able to make it. I took a quick shower, as the vomiting and the discovery made me all sweaty. I needed to get a grip, but it was hard, given the circumstances. Questions were going through my mind as I showered and dressed into jeans and a polo. What the hell is she doing in Montana—I thought she was closer to Colorado, but then everything from Detective Crane was a sham. Why a roastery? Why couldn't she just pick up the phone and call me? Why after all this time, hadn't she called or tried to contact me? My confusion turned to anger. How could she let me go through all of this?

I splashed ice cold water on my face. It's got to be that something is wrong. She wouldn't put me through the anguish unless something was very wrong and she couldn't contact me. But for this long? Just stop. Shake it out, grab the notebook, bring the card. Keep it simple. Don't jump to conclusions, don't let this thing win. You are in control. So I think, as I almost leave without my keys.

———

Ed is already at a booth and flags me down. He even has a beer waiting for me. Nice. But I'm only having one. A couple minutes later, Jay joins us, and after he orders his beer, we are ready to get down to business.

"Remember me telling you about the orange sticker missing from the supposed suitcase of Mara's?" I start.

They nod, and I pull out the card. "Check this out. Jill at Espresso

Yourself gave this to me two or three weeks ago. What do you see?" I give them some time to review it and then Jay pipes up, "Holy shit, there is an orange smiley face in the corner."

"Exactly. I'm thinking Mara took a chance to reach me or at least someone familiar, trying to be super subtle about it."

"Definitely subtle. Would you have thought it was her if you hadn't made the luggage discovery?" Ed asks.

Pausing, hating to admit this, I admit, "Probably not."

"So, could it still be coincidental?"

"Of course. But we know the 'accident' happened somewhere in the mountain region, and this is from Montana. Why go through this elaborate thing involving the coffee shop?" I reply.

Jay gets a concerned look on his face. "Because when you have very little to work with, and there is a lot of risk, you try to be as subtle as possible. And because you have no room to make a mistake."

"Absolutely, but as John just said, if he hadn't figured out the luggage thing, he wouldn't have thought twice about the card. He might have even thrown it away."

"Except Jill gave it to me."

"Again, a coincidence, you think you're her only favorite customer?" Jay inquired.

"No," I replied flatly, losing my excitement at the notion that Mara and I are so close, her thoughts would transcend.

"I'm not knocking it off completely, but we don't want to be heading down a wrong path," Jay said.

We sat in silence, each of us pondering what to do or say next. Breaking the silence, Ed piped up, "So let's do a little research on this roastery."

"Can't hurt," Jay replied. "Write down the name of the place and the address and I'll do a little digging tonight. In the meantime, send that card in, but put Mallory's name on it. This guy might be on the receiving end of it, and we don't want to potentially make things worse if we have it coming from John."

"Good idea. And then what?" I asked.

"Let me do my magic. If it is going to Montana, it's going to take a few days to get there. Just be cool and keep doing your daily thing," Jay instructed.

"How about all of us get together at my place Friday night? We can review Jay's findings. I'll even grill," I offered.

"Um, how about we go to your place, but I grill. You suck. Every burger you have ever made for me has been burnt," Ed teased.

"Whatever, jerk." I laughed. "Friday night it is."
"To Mara," Jay toasted. "To Mara," we toasted back.

Todd

Part of me feels vindicated and yet still somewhat unsatisfied. I thought Mara would've tried something desperate and stupid by now, thus giving me the final justification. Maybe it will have to be enough that she has been broken and now lives a life not of her choosing, just like I have had to live. Especially now that I know John appears to have moved on with his life.

It's what she deserves. She stole my chance at happiness. She destroyed what could have been a beautiful life with children around us, family meals, proudly going to church each week. A family that revered and loved me. She stole it all. It is what she deserves. And yet, there is a feeling of flatness.

The last letter and the photos should have provided a triumphant feeling—a feeling that I won. That her judgement and sentence, her misery, and the hollowness of her new life should be enough. She made me this way. And yet, the climatic victory doesn't feel like winning a game of chess with a worthy opponent.

She never was an equal adversary. Perhaps that is why there isn't joy. The best I have felt in all of this is that I have had my revenge. It has taken so long to get here, and I have savored it, but now what? All these years to get to now, and I have forgotten to see beyond it. What is my purpose now? She has accepted her fate, John has moved on, and frankly, all the watching has become tedious and boring. I should just take solace in the fact that my patience paid off, and God awarded me the win.

Perhaps now I can let go of this and truly dedicate myself to finding a proper wife. A man can be a father at any age. I am only forty. Many men my age have found a suitable submissive wife, young enough to still be fertile, who dedicate themselves to their husbands. I could be released from the illegal and yet necessary acts to make all this possible and take my skills into something more financially advantageous, to ensure that my future wife would never think she needed to work. I think it is time.

One more view into the life of John, and then I will turn it all off, disable all the cameras, the phone interceptors, destroy all the equipment, and then I'll start looking into what great new adventures I can turn my life toward. The last laugh is now mine, Mara. Enjoy your pathetic life.

I turn on camera five, located in a tree that shows me the front of John's house. Looks like a little soiree is in order. Maybe an engagement party. Four cars parked in front of the house. Two couples coming out of their cars. On the pathway to the door are two women, holding hands. How disgusting. This world has become so evil, society accepting homosexuality the way it has. I hope God destroys every one of them. The woman on the left is turning her head back over her shoulder.

Wait a minute. It can't be. This is wrong. I put the camera in reverse, zoom in on the face. NO!!!! It's the woman who was passionately kissing John. I thought they were lovers. I forward the tape, and now seeing her giving a kiss to the other woman and then a high five to John as they walk in the door.

I have been played. It was all a sham. That bitch. She got to John somehow. How could have I let my guard down for one minute? And John, he'll get his. All of them, all of them will die by my hand. Why would you let this happen, God? I've been patient. I GAVE UP EVERYTHING!

In a rage, I throw the monitors to the ground and throw the mouse against the wall. There is broken screen glass and plastic shards everywhere. THIS ISN'T FAIR!!!!!! The hate fills me, choking me in sobs, and violence. There is blood streaming out of my hands. I tear at my shirt, clawing at my chest. You will pay, Mara, oh, how you will pay.

Mara

The day started out as most of them do: I wake up, I make coffee, I do one household chore, I eat breakfast, I shower, and then I go to work and escape the compounding noise of only the thoughts in my head. Sometimes, I forget the sound of my mother's voice, I forget what the nieces and nephews look like, I cannot remember the color of every room in my house. I cannot remember what trees are in my backyard. I cannot recall what things are on my desk at the newspaper, what photos are there, what knickknack necessities are in my drawer, or even what coffee cup has residency.

What I never ever forget is John's cologne, what his kisses feel like, and how bare my hand is without my wedding ring. It is like there is a permanent indenture where it has sat for so many years. I am substantiated by memories; they are the only things that keep me glued together. I couldn't imagine if I had amnesia, what a horrible existence, worse I think than dementia. With dementia you don't know you have it. With amnesia, you know you are missing something, everything.

But if I start to dwell on it, I will only become awash with sadness, frustration, resentment, and potentially, hopelessness. Each day I'm at the office, I take on as much as possible so I'm not frantically pacing, waiting for the mailman and the possibility a survey card has returned. Day after day, nothing. But I have sent the 5-pound bag of beans anyway. Jill deserves it, and I don't want her calling, as right now, I don't want her to recognize my voice.

As I throw my jacket over my desk chair, I see my email inbox has several orders to process. I'm glad of it, and equally glad for Damon. He deserves this success, and being part of it is the beacon of light that makes this life here tolerable. I cannot believe my good luck in finding him. I don't think I would have been able to keep up the front at the restaurant. Being cheerful for several hours at a time takes a lot of work. Here, at least, Damon isn't in every day and I don't have to attempt sincere small talk. Not that I mind talking to Damon, it's just that some days it is hard, knowing how awesome his life is, while mine is a sham. I know it is temporary, but occasionally, it is easier to have a pity party. Shut up, Mara, and go get a cup of coffee.

Thankfully, it has been a busy morning, and I'm surprised when the mailman walks in the door with a decent stack held together by a thick rubber band. He gratefully takes the cup of coffee that I have for him, as there is quite a chill in the air.

"Thanks, Anne, I sure do appreciate it. So much better than that gut rot they have at the Post Office," he says.

"It is our pleasure, you just keep telling everyone where you got it," I reply with a genuine smile. George is a sweet old guy. I think he still delivers the mail as a means of staying in contact with people. He became a widow, I think, about five or six years ago.

I take the stack to my desk to sort. Bills in one pile for me, a few orders for me, a few items for Damon, and the usual barrage of circulars. And then it drops to the floor—a survey card. I'm hesitant to flip it over to see where it came from, for fear of being disappointed again. Five-star ratings across the board, nice. The return name is Mallory Allison Ramierez Ackley. From Minneapolis. From Espresso Yourself. I look at the name again and my heart skips a beat. It's from John. Because the name is my sister-in-law's, which includes her husband's name and her mother-in-law's maiden name, which if you take the first letters is MARA. ME!!!!! I let out several whoops of joy. Oh, my clever husband! He knows I'm alive! He got it! I knew he would!

My heart is racing madly and thousands of thoughts start popping into my head. How do I communicate further with him? How do I let him know about Todd? Should I just call Espresso Yourself and ask them to get a message to John? Should I come clean with Damon? Is it possible my imprisonment is soon to end? Would John come for me? But if he does, I need to let him know it might be dangerous to do so. How would I do that?

I hear the door open, and I peer out to see that it is Damon. I don't know if I should be calm and cool and say nothing or open up and tell him everything.

"Hey, Anne. How's it going this morning?" he asks cheerfully.

"Um, great. Been busy with quite a few online orders and we had a stack of mail, primarily junk, but it looks like you got a statement from the accountant. I put the relevant stuff on your desk."

"Cool. I'm not going to be here too long. I've got a day trip planned with Emma and the kids. We're off to find fossils for the kids' science class," he replies, using air quotes around "science class."

"That sounds like fun. Before you go, I think you should look at Roaster 1. There is some weird noise coming from the motor."

He riffles through the mail and turns to me. "Let's take a quick peek. If it is something beyond my ability, let's just call in the repair guy."

We walk over to the machine with a big plastic tub and a roll of paper towels. We'll need to clean out the basket on top and remove it in order to get to the motor. Coffee beans have a natural oil that leaves a residue and can gunk things up from time to time. We clean it after each batch to ensure the purity of flavor, but it can never be perfect.

We spend the next half hour cleaning and removing the basket. It appears that the motor needs to be taken apart, as there was nothing clogging it. "Well, bummer. Go ahead and call the repair guy in. I don't want to risk messing it up any further. How many orders do we have for this batch?"

"We are okay. I filled what we need now yesterday afternoon. I know there are a couple more orders, but if I can get Tommy in here today or tomorrow morning, we should be fine."

"Awesome," Damon answers as he wipes his hands with the paper towels. "I'll leave you a signed check. Tell him if he gets here this afternoon, I'll give him an extra fifty bucks."

I smile, it's just like Damon to get what he wants without being a demanding prick, yet taking care of people who solve his problems. "Dialing him up now."

After placing the call to Tommy, who had no problem coming in a couple of hours, I head back to my desk to plan out the roasting schedule for the orders that came in this morning. I don't have time right now to think of the next moves, I need to be alone when that happens.

We hear the bells jingle from the door being opened. We both walk to the front, and I turn pale.

"Good morning, sir. Are you the owner of this establishment?"

"Yes, I am. How can I help Agent . . .?"

"Agent Jackson from the Mountain Regional Office of the FBI. I have a warrant for the arrest of Mara Riley-Finegan."

"There's no one here by that name," Damon replies with a mystified look on his face.

"I'm sorry to tell you, sir, but this young lady here is our suspect. I'm guessing she told you her name was something else?"

The hurt, astonishment, and confusion is all over Damon's face. "You have to be wrong, Agent Jackson. This is Anne Howard, and she has been an employee of mine for close to a year. I did all the proper vetting." He shoots me a look. "That is the truth, isn't it, Anne?"

I'm stumbling to figure out what to say, so I go on the defensive. "This is no FBI agent, Damon. He's an imposter. He took me from my life in Minneapolis and has been keeping me captive here ever since."

Agent Jackson laughs. "Good one, Mara. How are you being held prisoner when you seem to go around this town as you please? I am sorry, sir, but I am taking her into custody."

Damon is at a loss, but he wants to believe this isn't happening. "What is she being arrested for?"

Agent Jackson pulls out a document and reads from it, "Mara Riley-Finegan, you are under arrest for the murder of your husband, John Finegan, for the embezzlement of funds from the Bank of Minneapolis in the amount of $2 million dollars, and for tax evasion. Agent Dawson, please handcuff Ms. Riley-Finegan and read her Miranda rights."

I plead with Damon, resisting being handcuffed. "Yes, Mara Riley-Finegan is my name, but I did not kill my husband. This imposter threatened me with killing John if I made any attempt to contact him. He is dangerous and should not be trusted. You should call the police right now."

"Ms. Riley-Finegan, if you continue resisting, we will have to use force. Stand down," Agent Dawson commands.

Agent Jackson just shakes his head, chuckling, "Ah, the stories criminals tell. I am just so sorry that you had to deal with her, sir."

"I am not sure what to believe. Anne, Mara, whatever, you've taken care of my kids. I trusted you with my business. Is this true?"

"No! I was forced to take on this identity. HE'S the one that set all this up. HE'S the criminal, please, I beg you. I'll give you John's number and you can call him, and you'll hear that he is alive."

"Nice try. Get her in the car. Sir, I'm grateful to see that no harm came to you and your family from this slick one. Thank you for your cooperation."

And as I'm shoved out the door by Agent Dawson, who really is Todd's bitch, Matt, I look back and see Damon slumped in his chair.

"Why are you here, Todd? I've done nothing to cause this. You jackass, why did you need to involve Damon? He's a good guy. Get these frigging handcuffs off me!"

"Mara, I have to admit, I was getting bored. I was seriously considering letting this end when I saw your husband getting passionate with a young lady, the one in the pictures I sent to you," Todd replies, then his tone became dark. "But then I see your gang all going to the house for what appeared to be a party, and that woman is holding hands and kissing another woman. I then realized I had been duped. I give the two of you credit. But I must know, how did you get to him without me noticing?"

I see that we are pulling into the driveway of the house I have been living in.

Ignoring his question, I ask, "What are you going to do?"

"Oh no, dear Mara, you don't get to ask questions, but you will answer mine."

The door opens and he grabs my arm tightly, practically yanking me out of the car, my arm socket strained. Still with the handcuffs on, he shoves me inside the house.

"Tie her up," he orders Matt. Matt has a gleeful look on his face as he wraps the rope around my arms, damn near cutting off the circulation, then removing the handcuffs. The rope around my ankles is cutting into my skin, causing me to wince in pain. I understand more is coming, so I brace for it, as I let my rage come to the surface.

"I asked you once, Mara, and I'll ask a final time. How did you get to John?"

Eyes blazing, I retort, "What does it matter, you sad pathetic freak?! He knows, and he is coming for me."

Todd pulls a chair in front of me, smirking, "Are you sure Mara? Are you sure I haven't already taken him out, as I told you I would?"

Fear that has kept me prisoner for this long, creeps into my chest, but I've come this far, I cannot let it win. "I'm sure. I'm as sure as the night is dark. You may be a lot of things, but a murderer, you aren't. I don't believe your faith or whatever you call it, would let you."

And there's the tell—the microscopic squint of his eyes. I remember this, as it happens every time he gets angry.

"Don't count on it. You don't know me anymore, and you are in no position to talk about faith, you stupid whore."

"That's it, Todd. Let's both just have it out, be angry, call each other names. Or better yet, have your bitch remove the ropes and let's just fight it out. I'd love to break your nose too," I sneer, looking back at Matt.

He snickers. "That is quite amusing, Mara. But I'm not going to engage in your savagery. I shouldn't be surprised. The wilderness has definitely made you less civilized."

"Super. Then how about you just let me go and we call this dumb game over?"

A darkness is now cast over his face. "I don't think so, Mara. You still broke the rules. There will still be consequences. John still dies, but not by my hand, by yours. You see, come Monday morning, you and John will be found at his office. He will be dead, and the weapon will be in your hand. You will be covered in his blood and will be awaking from your drug-induced sleep at just about the time the police arrive. You should have followed the rules, Mara. You could've accepted this beautiful place as your new home, but instead you will spend the rest of your life in prison. None of your family, John's family, or your friends will believe you, as the evidence of your other crime will be at the scene as well. I'll have long departed with the money you stole and have a grand life in the islands, while you rot."

I'm stupefied by his statement, my mind quickly trying to figure out how to stop all of this, but I can't. The fear that I thought I had under control overtakes me, and all I can do is silently choke on it.

John

It's been a long time since the last time I was in Montana. I forgot how stunning and how cold it is, but a different cold than Minneapolis. It is like touching plumbing— damp with the taste of iron in the air. The trees are all crystalized, twinkling as rays of the distant sun touch the limbs. As Jay and I enter Gardiner, the town seems a little brighter, less shabby. A touch of city life, and only a touch, has made it ten times more modern looking than the last time I was here.

We tried to do a Google Maps search of the Roastery as we drove in, but it couldn't be found. Guess Google hadn't quite made it here yet. Jay parked his SUV, leaving the motor running, and approached a Native American woman as she was getting into her pickup truck.

"Ma'am, hope I didn't startle you, but I just got into town and I am trying to find the Roastery."

The woman gave him a small smile. "You didn't startle, and it is one mile south. At the next light, turn right, and you will run into it. Good place, good people run it."

"Thank you so much, have a great day."

"It is my pleasure. Welcome to Gardiner. I hope you find what you are looking for," she said. "In your free time, stop on over to my shop for a visit. Here's my card."

Jay read the card out loud, "Ellen Whitehair, Native American Specialties. Thank you, Ms. Whitehair. My wife would love it if I brought back a good blanket."

She nodded and Jay hopped back into the SUV, backed out, and headed toward the stoplight. "John, just remember, we don't know what we are walking into. We don't know if this is a good or a hostile place."

"The lady back there said it was good people. I can trust that," I replied.

"I'm just saying we need to be cool and not emotional."

But I couldn't help it. I haven't slept much at all over the last couple days of driving, anticipating seeing my bride again. Of course, that was countered with all the dreadful possibilities as well. Did she want to see me? Maybe she preferred this life in Montana without me. But then why go through all the trouble to disappear? And why, after all this time, go through all the trouble to contact me so indirectly? Something was clearly very wrong about all of this if she had to go to such extreme and secretive measures to get a message to me.

As we arrived, it was all I could do to not just jump out the SUV and run to the front door. I strained to let Jay take the lead. The door jingled as we opened it, and there was a man sitting in a chair with a very tight expression on his face. He initially did not notice us entering, but as soon as he looked up, he put on a labored smile.

"Good afternoon, I'm Damon Richards, owner. What can I help you gentlemen with?"

Showing none of the restraint Jay asked me to have, I blurted, "Do you know a Mara Riley-Finegan?"

Damon turned right angry. "What the hell is going on here? Less than thirty minutes ago, the damn FBI showed up and took this Mara Riley-Finegan, who I thought was Anne Howard, and arrested her!"

Jay took his left hand and shoved me over. "The FBI? For what? What office did they say they were from? Did they show you identification?"

"Hey. You don't get to just walk in my business and start being demanding with me. Who the hell are you two?"

I whipped out my wallet. "I'm John Finegan, Mara's husband. She's been missing for over a year, and all leads brought us here. Please help us."

Damon carefully looked at my ID, as I continued, "This is my brother-in-law, Jay Ramierez. He's a Navy Seal, I promise you, we are the real deal."

"The two men said they were from the Mountain Regional Office of the FBI. Agent Jackson was the one that seemed in charge. I can't remember the name of the other guy."

Jay was texted furiously, and after a few minutes, "There is no Mountain Regional Office of the FBI, and no Agent Jackson. I just had one of my buddies check it out."

Damon covered his face with his hands. "My god, what have I done?"

"What do you mean?" Jay asked.

"The two agents, or imposters, handcuffed her, saying she was wanted for embezzling from the Bank of Minneapolis and murdering John . . . I guess that would be you . . . John Finegan. I am such an idiot."

Jay quickly reassured him, "Don't beat yourself up, but this does mean that Mara is in danger and that bank is going to get robbed, if it hasn't been already. Where did they go?"

"I have no idea," he replied.

I started to panic, but I was trying to squash it. "Do you know where she has been living?"

"Sure, I've taken her home several times," he responded.

My eyes widened. Reading my expression, Damon quickly responded, "Oh, not like 'take her home.' I'm very happily married with too many kids. Anne, I mean Mara, has become family. She has a great relationship with my wife, Emma, and she does some English tutoring for my kids."

Jay jumped in. "Okay, great. Damon, can you please tell us where she is living?"

"I'll take you there myself. Let me grab my keys and let's get going. Should I call the sheriff?"

"Not yet, we don't want any sirens to alert them. I'm fine with you taking the lead, but I want you to find a spot several hundred yards from the house, as we need to be stealthy in our approach. In fact, once we get there, I want you to stay in your car."

"The hell I am," Damon responded as he pulled out a gun from his desk drawer, checking the safety and the cartridge.

"Nice Glock, I take it you're licensed to carry it?" Jay asked.

"Absolutely, I just got this G17L about a year ago. You don't live in Montana without a few choice weapons."

Jay nodded, and I gave them both a look, pleading them to quit yapping and let's go. "Yep, we are going to head out, but we need to have a couple plans in place," he said. "There are only two guys, right, Damon?"

"Yes, the one who did all of the talking was medium build, nothing unique about him, but the other guy is a little over six foot and fairly good sized," Damon added.

"Size doesn't mean much, it's how quick a guy is, how well-trained he is, that determines what we are up against. As we don't know anything about either of their abilities, we will need to assume they are formidable."

We took a few more minutes to discuss the layout of the house, the hill, the road leading up to the house, and how we were going to approach it. Damon made a quick call to his wife Emma, telling her he was going to be delayed and to go on ahead to wherever she was going without him.

"I just don't want her to worry about anything," he said almost apologetically.

"Hey, given the situation, I understand completely," I told him.

While Damon was locking up the shop, Jay went to the back of his SUV and the secret storage space underneath the carpet. In it was a variety of weapons, and he pulled out a gun for me. "I assume you are also updated on your licenses?"

I looked at the Sig Sauer and confirmed that my permit to carry was updated. I didn't even think to pack my own handgun, which is locked up in the safe at home. This was another benefit to having Jay as my brother-in-law. He handed the gun to me after checking the safety and loading a new cartridge into it. I'm no expert like Jay, but hanging around him and Sean led me to make the decision to have a gun. They occasionally take me with them to the gun range for practice, which is fun and empowering. Obviously, I cleared it with Mara first, but now I want to kick myself for not insisting that she get trained as well.

"John. Earth to John. Your head on?" Jay inquired.

"Yes, sorry, just thinking."

"It's going to be okay. I promise. I'm going to ride with Damon and you follow in the SUV. That way I can better determine where to park the cars."

Damon piped up, "We'll need to park tightly on the side of the road. The house is up a hill but the road is gravel and not very wide."

"We'll park in the grasses, if need be," Jay replied.

"That's illegal. It's still considered park land."

"I'll deal with it."

We loaded up in our respective vehicles, Damon equipped with my cell phone number in case he needed to text me. I closed my eyes, exhaled, took one big gulp of coffee, and started the SUV.

Mara

"So now what? We're just going to have some bonding time?" I ask defiantly, trying to remain in control of my fear.

I can hear Matt rummaging through the fridge and cabinets. "Good grief, woman, don't you have anything to eat around here?" he asks.

I don't reply, but Todd does, "Matt, pull in the cooler from the car, I've plenty of provisions for the next several days."

I'm at a loss. "What the hell for, I thought we were heading to Minneapolis?"

"Mara, that mouth of yours. Please don't force me to tape it shut. I'm waiting a couple of days to ensure the coast is clear, that everything else is in place before we fly back to Minneapolis."

"I need to use the bathroom."

"Not a problem. But if you don't follow exactly what I tell you, then next time, you can sit in your own mess. I will untie you, you move your arms to the front, I'll handcuff you again, and then you can go. The window is sealed shut, and there is nothing in there but toilet paper. Are we clear?"

"Crystal."

I scrounge through the bathroom's medicine cabinet and the small linen closet. Damnit, everything is gone. There is nothing in here but one hand towel, soap, and toilet paper. Nothing I can use. No means of escaping yet. No means of getting another message to John. I start silently crying for a minute or two.

"Let's go, Mara. There's nothing to find in there," Todd calls out.

I rinse my face, as I'm sure as hell not going to let him know I was crying, and then make my way out of the bathroom, still in handcuffs. "Little hard to do my business handcuffed like this."

"Too bad," he says, while looking at his laptop. "We really should have provided better Wi-Fi here, little slow. Must be annoying, but then all you have is time, right, Mara?"

"Fuck off," I mutter under my breath.

He pops out of his chair and slaps me across the face. "Are you just stupid? How many times have I told you that I will not tolerate that language?"

"Fuck you, fuck your pathetic spineless mother, fuck your rapist gorilla fucking father, and fuck every blood relation in your fucking family," I shout, knowing full well this will only infuriate him more. And it does, as his backhand blows against the other side of my face.

"Enough!" He gets into my face. "Let's be clear, Mara. It absolutely will get worse for you. The next will be a fist, not an open hand."

Stinging from the slap, I smile as brightly as possible. "Is that what your daddy did? Just hit you every time you couldn't be a man in his eyes? Poor, sad, little Todd."

The next thing I know, I'm lying on the ground, seeing stars with the taste of blood covering my tongue, pouring out of my mouth. Though I'm in pain, I feel a sense of great pleasure at knowing I've touched a sore spot with him.

"Keep talking, Mara, and I promise you won't recognize your face in the mirror!" he shouts.

I wobbly crawl up to the chair, still in handcuffs. "What does it matter? You're going to kill me anyway."

"No, no, dear one, you aren't going to die. John is, remember? And he is going to see it coming, with you lying at his feet. If you don't want him to recognize you as he remembers you, by all means, keep talking."

The thought of John dead makes me shudder, and I decide to keep quiet. Not that I care anymore if he hits me because I don't believe I'll be alive in the end. But knowing that I'll be responsible for John's death makes me sick. Mentally, I pray to God for an answer, for a way out, but it is only the sound of Todd clicking away at the laptop and Matt's disgusting chewing that I hear.

John

We parked at least a three hundred yards away, one car on each side of the road in the thick of the tall wild grasses. I never did turn around to see what I imaged would be a spectacular view of the mountains and the town. All I could see is Mara's face, all I could hear was the loud thumping of my heart, and all I could taste was the salty beads of sweat trickling down my face.

Per Jay's orders, we all slunk down in the tall grasses. Jay and I on the right side, Damon behind us on the left side. Jay motioned to Damon, and he gave back the okay hand signal—I can only imagine he was just as nervous as I was. The front of the house had three steps to a small porch with a door a few feet deeper. On each side of the steps was a solid wall with pretty flowers covering the cracked stucco. Surely that was Mara's doing.

After what seemed like hours, Jay signaled for Damon to slither up to the left side of the steps and crouch as tightly as he could up against the wall. As agreed, I was to cover the back of the house and wait for Jay to yell "Breach" before coming in the back door. Jay was going to quietly pull himself up the right side of the porch and ease his way to the door, out of view of the one front window that was covered by a thin curtain.

Every small crackle of dead grass seemed as loud as an explosion. Jay had told us to be careful not to let it unnerve us, as animals were always roaming around. He reminded us that the noise was part of the landscape. It still unhinged me. Before I cleared the side of the house, I saw Damon was in his position and that Jay had made it up the porch without setting off any alarms. I quickly made my way to the back. Thankfully, there were no steps to climb.

I positioned myself under the window of the storm door. I couldn't hear anything inside the house but a couple muffled voices, none of which seemed female. It took every ounce of will power to fight the anxiety of helplessness, but I was not going to fail. I was not going to lose her again.

Jay

Seeing John make his way to the back and Damon securely in his spot, I silently counted to thirty, giving John time to get in place. I have done hundreds of frontal assaults before, in way more difficult scenarios, but this time it was personal. When it is personal, it becomes even more imperative to shut it down and stay true to what I knew, not what I felt.

I knelt just to the right of the one window on the left of the door, so only my right eye was at the corner, looking inside. Mara was sitting in a chair, blood dripping from the edge of her mouth; one man was sitting at a table, cutting into something on his plate; another man was sitting with his back to me, typing on a laptop. This was good.

I inhaled deeply, measured my heart rate, and turned all my focus to the mission at hand. My right hand pulled out the gun, my left hand behind me doing a finger countdown for Damon: three, two, one.

I smashed the door in and Damon hopped up behind me. I pointed my gun at the guy who was at the table but who had, with an amazing quickness, yanked Mara out of the chair. He now had an arm around her with a knife at her throat. Damon pointed his gun at him, as I had mine pointed at the man with the laptop, who, with equal speed, had a gun pointed at me.

I had told Damon to just start yelling, as I started yelling, to create confusion, "Drop the knife, asshole, or he will put a bullet in your head!"

We all stood like statues in our positions. I wished I had taken the guy holding Mara because I knew I could easily take him out before he flicked his wrist with the knife. I silently chided myself for this error. Damon stood solid, which made me feel only slightly better.

The man with the laptop spoke first, strangely and very calmly, "Neither Matt nor I will have any issue slicing her throat. There will be no surrender."

I could tell we had surprised them, but obviously they were trained as well. There were no amateurs here except Damon and John.

He continued, "Damon, it is unfortunate that you got involved. You should have just stayed at your shop. Before I leave here, I will make sure your beautiful wife and children will all be sacrificial lambs."

"Ignore him, Damon. He's buying time," I warn. But it must have hit a primal part of every father and husband. He started shaking. Shit.

"You must be the asswipe named Todd. Pull your dog off and no one will get hurt," I said.

The big guy named Matt just barely moved the hand holding the knife against Mara's throat, and then all hell ensued. Damon let off a shot, then Todd let off a shot and bolted to the back. "DAMNIT! BREACH! JOHN, BREACH!" I quickly looked behind me and saw Mara and Matt on the floor and Damon standing over both of them with his gun still pointed at Matt. I didn't waste time figuring out what happened. I bolted toward the back, trying to overtake Todd. The back door crashed open.

John knocked Todd over, and I caught up with him and pulled Todd up on his feet. I backed away a foot, just to the left. John had his gun up against Todd's forehead, while Todd still had his gun lowered at his side.

"DROP THE GUN!" I yelled, but Todd wouldn't comply. "John, back away, I have him. Back away!"

But he wouldn't. Then for a second, he looked back down the hallway, past me, seeing Damon over the two bodies. As if in slow motion, I followed his gaze, saw the blood on the floor. John's face crinkled into a rage I had never seen on him before but had seen all too often on a defeated enemy.

"WHY?!" he screamed, as I simultaneously screamed, "NO!"

And then there was only the deafening sound of gunshot.

Epilogue

After some time in the ambulance and a couple days talking to the police, sorting out all the details, I was released and drove back to Minneapolis. There were no funerals and no graveside services in the days that followed. I spent time trying to shake off the series of events that had happened. As this was personal, this was tougher than most of my missions.

I probably will never forget the look on John's face when he saw Mara on the floor. It is an expression of one who has nothing left to lose, and it is dangerous. Mara is part of John's tapestry, his brain, heart, and soul. Losing Mara again would snap the ties that bind, and there would only be a shell of a man remaining. The last thing that needed to happen was John going to jail.

But as I snapped my head back toward him, the gun went off. The ringing was so sharp in my ears, and I saw that John moved his aim from Todd's forehead to the wall. The noise was deafening, and Todd doubled over, painfully grasping his ear, most likely with a shattered eardrum. I shook my head, as the noise affected me too, and saw a defiant John standing over Todd.

"If it is possible to find a way to cause as much pain to you as you have caused me, I'd love to find it. I'm letting you live because you will spend the rest of your life in jail, never walking in the light, and that will be more satisfying than killing you," John uttered in a soft but sturdy voice.

I couldn't believe it. I'm trained to endure the emotional and psychological torture a potential captor might invoke, but John wasn't. Any normal human being would have killed Todd. I knocked the gun out of Todd's hand and kicked it away, as John climbed over him and ran to the living room. I pulled out my phone and called 911, requesting both police and an ambulance. I then roughly pulled Todd up off the floor and pushed him into a dining room chair, gun still pointed at him.

"Damon, lower your gun and tie this guy up," I instructed as I joined John on the floor. The big guy, Matt, was rolling in pain, as it appeared Damon shot him in the leg, but my only concern was with Mara.

John was shaking as he hovered over her body. I gently moved him aside slightly so I could check for a pulse. "John, she's alive!" I exclaimed joyously.

It didn't quite register with him, given the shock of the last few minutes. He was sobbing and wiping away tears, kissing her face frantically. I quickly scanned her body for any potential gun wounds but there weren't any, thankfully. She must have been knocked unconscious from falling to the ground. After a few seconds, her eyes fluttered open. Forgetting she was handcuffed, she hit herself in the face when she attempted to rub her eyes.

I couldn't help but giggle. I know, that sounds terrible, but in those last horrible minutes, I thought that our worlds had crashed, and her clumsy move made me laugh.

John and I each grabbed an arm so she could sit up. Matt was groaning in pain, and well, I couldn't help myself, I punched him so he would just shut up. For a moment I forgot about Damon guarding Todd. I got up and took over, as Damon gratefully collapsed in the other chair.

"Holy shit, how did this all happen so fast?" he asked.

"Your reflexes took over when you saw him move his wrist against Mara's throat. That was impressive, that you got him in the leg and somehow didn't hit Mara."

"Pure luck. Pure crazy ass luck," he replied.

At the sound of sirens approaching, I let out a sigh of relief and smiled, watching John cradle Mara's head, arms wrapped around her, never to let her go ever again.

ABOUT THE AUTHOR

Lisa Landis is originally from Iowa, lives in Minneapolis with her partner in all things, Eric. She is the mom of "K" who will become an endless source of information for future books as a forensic scientist; and of her beloved three-legged Bernese Mountain Dog, Diva.

Disappear is Landis' second novel; her first novel *Waiting*, can be found under her previous name, Lisa Landis Dolan.